P9-DIE-956

WILD
BLUES

Beth Kephart

WILD BLUES

A CAITLYN DLOUHY BOOK

Atheneum Books for Young Readers

New York   London   Toronto   Sydney   New Delhi

East Bridgewater Public Library
32 Union Street
East Bridgewater, MA 02333

atheneum

ATHENEUM BOOKS FOR YOUNG READERS
An imprint of Simon & Schuster Children's Publishing Division
1230 Avenue of the Americas, New York, New York 10020

This book is a work of fiction. Any references to historical events, real people, or real places are used fictitiously. Other names, characters, places, and events are products of the author's imagination, and any resemblance to actual events or places or persons, living or dead, is entirely coincidental.

Text copyright © 2018 by Beth Kephart
Jacket illustration copyright © 2018 by John Jay Cabuay
Interior illustrations copyright © 2018 by William Sulit
The quote on p. 75 is from Dan D'Imperio's *The ABCs of Victorian Antiques*.
All rights reserved, including the right of reproduction in whole or in part in any form.
ATHENEUM BOOKS FOR YOUNG READERS is a registered trademark of Simon & Schuster, Inc. Atheneum logo is a trademark of Simon & Schuster, Inc.

For information about special discounts for bulk purchases, please contact Simon & Schuster Special Sales at 1-866-506-1949 or business@simonandschuster.com.
The Simon & Schuster Speakers Bureau can bring authors to your live event. For more information or to book an event, contact the Simon & Schuster Speakers Bureau at 1-866-248-3049 or visit our website at www.simonspeakers.com.
Interior design by Vikki Sheatsley
The text for this book was set in Dante MT Std.
The illustrations for this book were digitally rendered.
Manufactured in the United States of America   0518 FFG
First Edition   10 9 8 7 6 5 4 3 2 1
Library of Congress Cataloging-in-Publication Data
Names: Kephart, Beth, author.
Title: Wild blues / Beth Kephart.
Description: First edition. | New York : Atheneum Books for Young Readers, [2018] | Summary: Thirteen-year-old Lizzie relates, through a victim statement, her harrowing journey through the Adirondacks seeking her disabled friend, Matias, who was kidnapped by escaped convicts.
Identifiers: LCCN 2017030035 | ISBN 9781481491532 (hardcover) | ISBN 9781481491556 (eBook)
Subjects: | CYAC: Adventure and adventurers—Fiction. | Missing children—Fiction. | Criminals—Fiction. | Victims of crimes—Fiction. | Dwarfs (Persons)—Fiction. | People with disabilities—Fiction. | Salvadoran Americans—Fiction. | Adirondack Mountains (N.Y.)—Fiction.
Classification: LCC PZ7.K438 Wil 2018 | DDC [Fic]—dc23
LC record available at https://lccn.loc.gov/2017030035

East Bridgewater Public Library
32 Union Street
East Bridgewater, MA 02333

In honor of Uncle Danny,
lost much too soon.
I miss you every day.

Pluck has carried many a girl* triumphantly through what seemed the forlornest hope.

—*The Art of Keppy,*

a rare find passed down by Uncle Davy

*As adapted by Lizzie, as encouraged by Mr. Genzler

WILD
BLUES

1

NOBODY IS JUST THEIR GENES, OR JUST THEIR proteins.

Nobody is only DNA.

I, for example, am Lizzie, pure Lizzie, and my uncle was my uncle and not the gossip people told, and my mother was my mom and not her cancer. We were all the all of who we were, and I'm going to tell my story straight through, and then, maybe then, you will tell yours. You will see how much it hurts to say the whole truth of who you are, plus the truth of all that happened.

This is a victim impact statement. Offered right here, from this bed, in this room, in this house, to you, because as you can see, I am not moving.

Another thing for this record, up front: Matias is a part of this story, and Matias was not his condition. So he had a problem with his pituitary gland. So it had turned his growth hormone off. So the only way

Matias had a chance of getting taller was by keeping to a schedule—an every-day shot of growth juice. All true. He'd had this done to him since he was small. He'd done it to himself since he was eight. Had gotten up each day and punched the needle in, but he was still so short, and he was running out of time. Matias wished for his shoes to grow small or his pants to grow short, but neither happened. He wished for a body that could run as fast as other bodies run.

He did not have a body that could run like that.

That body, that gland, is not who Matias was.

But some of that is part of this story.

You know a little. You were there. You played a part. You had firsthand news about the prison break down the road—the two men who popped up from a sewer hole with their hair combed back and their hello hands waving. The two men who were Hollywood inside their own heads, who were coming close to famous, who'd waited winter to spring to summer and now were on the move, and weren't just their DNA either, their genes.

Those two men had a choice.

They had an accomplice.

People ask me, was I afraid?

Not yet.

Not then.

But soon.

2

LET'S START IN SUNSHINE. LET'S START WITH the absolute true: My uncle was wild beauty in motion, and I was the one who knew. You couldn't trench a fence around him. Couldn't box him with a frame. He was in and out, there and here, a blaze of Day-Glo glory.

He loved me best. He told me so. I was his primo family. Which is why when Mom said, month before last, "Choose your summer adventure"—*choose*—I chose my uncle and his reno'ed schoolhouse cabin, his swatch of God's elastic earth, his way of laughing, which made me laugh, which made us both laugh harder. Anytime I got a choice, I always chose my uncle. I chose four highway hours north from here, one quick bump east, one cut up a diagonal road that quickly skinnied. I chose where the hills are almost mountains, and the trees are so green that the shade is black, and the loose gravel rattles the belly of the car.

And there are streams, and not just streams but something they call kettles.

I chose my uncle, which means I also chose my friend Matias. The three of us as indivisibles, or that's what I thought then.

Mom's hands were tight on the steering wheel. Her long black hair with its bright-white roots whipped around her head, tornado style.

"You ready?" she said.

I had my solo suitcase in the rear and my caterpillar backpack by my feet. I was wearing my turquoise Keens loose and my khaki shorts long to my knees. The bill of my Phillies cap was pointing back. I'd written emergency facts in the palms of both hands, and the ink was already sweating.

"Ready for anything," I said.

3

NO.

I'm sorry. I can't.

Won't, either.

That's running the story ahead of itself, and the rules are I tell you what happened. I tell it like I remember it happening, and you don't ask me questions. We already know, you especially know, what happens when rules get broken.

I'm at the start of this story, here with Mom. I'm on the road with the gravel, with the buzzy shade and the perky streams. Up ahead, in his schoolhouse cabin, Uncle Davy's waiting, breakfast-at-lunchtime on his barrel-bellied stove. In his own white house, like a snow-fort house, Matias is waiting too. His house is on a hill, and you can't see it for the trees.

"Someday I'll meet your Matias," Mom says, like she can read my thoughts through the silence between us.

"Could be."

"We'll have a picnic. We'll go hiking."

"Mom?"

"End of summer, I'll be better. I'll come for a Matias visit."

Biology is my best subject and my second-most-important hobby, and I know a lot about cells, by which I mean mutations, divisions, arrests, and yes, DNA and genes and proteins and heredity, which is not the same as inheritance. Mom doesn't know and I don't know if Mom is going to get better. I don't know, so I don't answer. I believe in truth.

"You'll keep my business as my business," Mom says after a bit. "Won't you, Lizzie?"

I nod.

"Including your uncle."

"Mom," I say.

"Some things are private."

I dip my chin. That is my yes. Mom's doctor news is just and only our news. That's the way she wants it.

The road ahead grows skinny. I see the log cabins in their tuck behind the slippery elms and the aspens quaking and the eastern hop hornbeams, trees I know the words for. I see the skirt of raw earth, and the bumpy road, and the acreage of empty in-betweens. I see the vending machine by the side of the road, left there like some pay phone.

You think a pay phone would have saved us?

You think you can know for sure?

You don't. You can't. Nobody can. And besides: This is my telling.

They say telling heals. I'm not persuaded. I don't know the honest what of my own healing, and ten days is all we have. I said yes to the lawyers, to telling this story, to giving you a chance to listen. Somebody said, but I forget who, that this will go down as your partial restitution. I looked that word up, "restitution." "An act of restoring or a condition of being restored," says *Merriam-Webster*. Also: "a making good of or giving an equivalent for some injury."

Making good? You think me telling you this story can make this good? Can make *us* good? I have my doubts, but I said yes, and mostly I play by the rules.

You're taller than I thought you'd be. Prettier, too, since I'm being honest. I see the daisies you brought and the Dixie cup you brought them in, and the daisies weren't expected. Rules are you stay until the fireflies fly in each night and not one single tock later.

I'll be watching for the blinks of light.

I'll be listening for the tock.

Mom is driving and the road gets skinny. That's how this starts. Mom is driving and the music of the mountains *is*, and her doctor news is too big for two, and I can't see far enough ahead.

4

FIRST THING THAT'S COMING INTO VIEW IS Uncle Davy's cabin—*was* coming into view, guess I should say. Back then. End of June. Red clapboard with white-trimmed windows, which were shaped like crescent moons. A tall violet door, because Uncle Davy was tall, and a doorknob the color of the sun. Three steps going up, a bunch of bushes to each side, garden goods popping from the earth out back, a little haze of butterflies, all of them, always, alive. And right out front, sitting low on the drive, was Uncle Davy's '69 Dodge Dart with its hitched-in trailer, which was painted black except for two white words: D'ERASIO COLLECTIBLES.

Mom cut in, pulled behind the Dart, and parked. She released the wheel, reached for my hand, kissed me on the cheek. I kissed her back, and all of a sudden I could picture her on her long, lonesome drive home, pulling up to the house, taking the medicine that waited, that would make her sick so that maybe she could get better, and I got an ache right hard inside my pulmonary action. You take pills like those and you're walking radiation. They say to wait it out alone. I say that really sucks.

"News for two," she said. "Don't forget?"

She had tears in her eyes, two brown-green pools that I was swimming in.

"Two," I said.

She looked past me then, and I turned and there was Uncle Davy hurrying out to the stoop, calling for me like he always did, waving halfway to my mother. A minor salute.

"Lizzie love," he said.

He was a TV star. I was his best and only niece. Mom was behind me, touching, I could guess, one hand to the tornado in her hair. Him. Me. Her. Us. Combinations of two, but not three.

You know what estrangement is? You know how it looks and how it sounds? Like a crack in an egg, like my mother and my uncle, the silence between them, the way they talked through me. I got out with my stuff. Mom reached for my hand. I turned back to face her. She brushed at a tear and said, "I love you," and I said, "I'll miss you," because sometimes you need only a couple of words and not all the words in the books to say everything you mean.

Mom looked for a quasi at my uncle, threw a mini of a salute, then stared straight ahead and unparked and waved for real at the brother she wasn't looking at. She gunned the car, turned onto the road, spun for a second, and was gone, and in four hours she'd be home, where all three stories of the narrow house were mostly empty, and where the world's worst word— "diagnosis"—was shivery in the shadows. Radiation iodine is not for sissies and it's not for sharing. Just ask the Nuclear Regulatory Commission.

"Lizzie!"

Uncle Davy had left the door to the cabin wide open, and I could see the whole insides from where I stood, everything like it always was: The downstairs trundle, where I'd sleep. The weird stove in the middle and the unwashed chalkboard and the kitchen table with the gingham cloth and the bowls and spoons and the basket of polished acorns, a celebrity preroga- tive, Uncle Davy said. I could see up the ladder, to the loft, to the bed where my uncle slept, which was gold, and the three silk pillows, which were raspberry fade.

Everything other was the flea market finds that had made my uncle famous.

Because my uncle and I, we were collectors. Him of the stuff that dead people made. Me of the stuff all around us. He liked stained-glass lamps and tasseled chairs and tin-toothed nutcracker soldiers. I liked rocks and butterflies, leaves and shells, pinecones and polished acorns. He had a name for everything he owned. I had a book and a pencil and a list and an idea that someday, somehow, I'd have a noun for every Earth thing I saw, I'd be world beloved for my supreme, impressive knowledge. My knowing everything would be a kind of cure.

"I'll be famous as you someday," I'd say to Uncle Davy, who was a guy who needed sunglasses big as turtle shells to go out in public. "Be careful what you wish for," he'd say back, because fame turns into stories, and stories into gossip, but I guess that's not something I need to tell you. I guess you know the fame facts well. I guess I've been distracted. Point is:

I loved my uncle true, and I was hugging him so hard that I almost lost my breath, and it was "Missed you," "Missed you," until his arms unclasped and we were walking side by side into that cabin, and my mother was driving away, driving away down that road. I threw my pack into one corner. I smelled the Cream of Wheat steaming on the stove. "Breakfast every time of day" was Uncle Davy's motto. I was four hours of traveling hungry and I was full of secret sorrows, and I was headed for the table.

"Holy Vogelzang," Uncle Davy said, looking past me, through a window.

I turned to see what he was seeing, but he was already out the door and down the steps in his slippery-soled shoes and yellow socks and navy trousers—he was running to the back of his reno'ed schoolhouse cabin with a turquoise-colored fly swatter in one hand. There are rocks out there and dewy grass, and that cabin sits on a hill, and my uncle is really tall and kind of spazzy—all wild beauty in motion, like I said. I had a bad feeling. I ran. Got around to the back in zipper time. In a single second, with my biology eyes, I saw the problem—a clump of garden rhubarb chomped right down to stubs. Food chain problems.

"Was planning on making you pie," Uncle Davy said, out of breath and still holding his swatter high. He was looking out beyond the small square of mowed backyard, past the bushes, toward the forest, and down the hill, where the white flags of deer tails were disappearing.

"Criminal element," he said, meaning the whitetails. And then he bent down and rubbed one knee, and then he stood up and he leaned his weight onto my shoulder, and we stood for a while staring at the chomped stubs, feeling the mountain air.

"I'm too old to be chasing deer," he said.

"You're a star," I said. "You shouldn't have to."

He laughed and I could see his twisted tooth. He straightened his hair, his trousers, his purple tie, and he was handsome. We started our walk back, his twisted knee giving him a funky limp.

"Was planning on making you a breakfast pie," he said.

"Would have been nice."

"You plant a garden for your favorite niece and you end up feeding Bambi."

"Way of the world," I said before I could stop me. "Way of the world." Words that belonged to my mom.

"How *is* your mom?" Uncle Davy asked.

"Mom?" I said. "You saw."

"She going to be okay?"

I nodded. I swallowed hard. "You need a fence," I said.

"A fence?"

"If you're serious about the rhubarb, you need a fence to stop the deer. Separate the species."

"I'm not a fence builder, Lizzie."

"Just telling you what Mr. Genzler would say."

"Mr. Genzler?"

"My biology mentor."

"Hmmm," he said. Then: "Wish we could all just get along."

"That would be nice."

"We'll buy a pie. We'll be just fine."

We walked slow. We took our time. I tried to see what was new about the place; it'd been a while since last time. The rocky earth still fell down, down. The birds still perched on the limbs of forest trees. The air was sweet, but then it wasn't. Uncle Davy smelled it first.

"Cream of Wheat," he said, a catch in his throat.

I smelled it now.

"Uncle Davy!"

I left him stranded and ran. Around the house, up the steps, into the one room of the old cabin, to the barrel-bellied stove, where the pot was scorched and smoking. I grabbed the kitchen mitts and then the pot and tossed the mess into the sink, turned on the spigot. If there had been fire alarms, they'd have been ringing. The smoke spewed thick as fog. Only thing I could see for a little while after that was my uncle's yellow socks and my uncle's turquoise swatter, knocking the smoke this way and that.

"Oh, Lizzie," Uncle Davy said, coughing. "I'm sorry."

"We're good," I said, keeping my voice real calm and my wits about me and my courage front and center, courage being my first and most important hobby, courage being the only choice we have, according to what Mr. Genzler says.

"First day here and you're putting out fires."

"I've seen worse," I said, "in bio lab. You should see Terrence Ridley with the Bunsen burner." The smoke was up in my lungs, my throat. My voice was squeaky. My eyes burned.

"That was going to be an excellent pot of wheat," my uncle said.

"The pot's wrecked," I said.

"Probably."

"The smoke . . ."

"Let's open windows."

He limped one way. I went the other. There was a lot of smoke, but there really hadn't been much fire, and we were together on this, with a plan.

"How old are you now?" my uncle asked after we'd done what we could do, after the mountain air was pushing in and the smoke was starting to clear. Asked it like he didn't know, like he'd never known, like he wasn't there the day I was born, back when Mom and him were still best of friends and told each other secrets.

"Thirteen."

"Remarkable," he said.

5

RULES ARE I DON'T HAVE TO ANSWER ANYTHING you ask, if you ask, but since you did and since it's up to me, all I'm saying is this: I learned my courage from my father. No. Not like you're saying. No. Nothing like that. No, he was no firefighter. No, he was no cop. He was . . . my father. He taught me—who *not* to be and how to stand up for myself and how to be strong for my mom.

I don't see my father. Haven't seen him. Wouldn't. I'm—I'm just saying that it was from my father that I learned my best and my most useful hobby, which is courage, and besides: Someone had to stop the fire.

There were eggs. I cracked and fried them. We kept the windows open and the violet door, too, and the smoke grew thin, and sometimes a dragonfly would zig its way into the cabin, then zig back out, and sometimes a squirrel would hop right up to the open door, then quit and go back to the forest where it had come from, and after a while we forgot about the fire, and the smell, and the Cream of Wheat, and the pie, and it was just the two of us, like it normally was, getting caught up on everything that wasn't private.

Uncle Davy gave me the news on his latest finds—a pair of chairs he called the mission and the Hunzinger. I reported on the admirals, swallowtails, and monarchs—the prettiest butterfly collection he could imagine. I'd pinned them to the mounting board, I said. I'd built the shadow boxes. I'd worked with Mr. Genzler as an after-school project, and no, I promised Uncle Davy, no butterflies had been killed for this assignment. Every butterfly we pinned was a stilled specimen we'd found in the school's garden.

"Stilled," Uncle Davy said.

"That's how Mr. Genzler puts it."

"Oh, the euphemisms," Uncle Davy said.

"Life is life," I said. "Until it's not."

Right about then was when I remembered the present I'd brought for Uncle Davy. "Close your eyes," I said, and he did. I walked to the backpack, unzipped, and dug in. I found what I wanted in no time. Shook it out. Smelled it for smoke. It had a stink, but not too bad.

"Guess," I said.

"Turquoise?" he said, thinking, I guess, of that swatter.

"Close," I said. "But not exactly."

I laid the gift on his lap. He opened his eyes. It was a brand-new, phenom Day-Glo apron. I'd made one each year in my home science class. This was the fourth in his collection.

"Lime green!" he said. "Close cousin to turquoise."

"My most spectacular creation as of right yet," I said. Because on a list of best and most important hobbies, home science was nowhere. Not a best. Not anything close. My Day-Glos, with their big-stitch hems and stringy strings, were my form of protest.

Uncle Davy rubbed his knee and then stood up. I tied his apron on. He looked terrific, with the lime green dangling crooked over his navy trousers, and his purple tie swinging above it.

"All right," Uncle Davy said. "Now one for you." He limped across the room, dug into an antique hutch, then limped back with a rectangular crush of tissue paper, no bow. I remembered, while I waited, the gifts of Uncle Davy's past. A Victorian shoehorn. A pearl-crusted frame. A sewing bird. A shaving mug. "Rare things for a rare bird," he'd always say, and now he was placing this new thing in my lap, and now we were back on track, as if there had never been a fire.

"A book?" I said.

"I'm not ruining the surprise."

I tore the tissue paper off and I was right: a sweet book with a pine-tree-green cover, its pages thin as Bible pages. Its illustrations were old-fashiony. Its lessons included "Getting Lost," "Pathfinding," "Nature's Guide Posts," and "Accidents and Emergencies." I closed the book again, stared down at its title. *Camping and Woodcraft*. Author: Horace Kephart.

"Found two copies at an estate sale. One for each of us," Uncle Davy said.

"For me?"

"For us."

"You're going to start camping now?"

"This is history, Lizzie. This is culture. Kephart was the Dean of American Campers. He was a mayor. He was the guy who helped create Great Smoky Mountains National Park. Fame, Lizzie. Fame. They even named a mountain after him. This is a find so fine it keeps its value on the shelf." He spoke like this kind of luck just never happened.

"I like it," I said.

"Courage," my uncle Davy said. "And biology. Like Kephart had you in mind when he wrote it."

"Me and Mr. Genzler," I said, imagining my uncle in a basement somewhere, finding the book in a cardboard box. Imagining Mr. Genzler, green with envy.

"I hereby christen you *The Art of Keppy*," I said to the book. *The Art of Keppy*, which trumps the real title anytime and sounds a bit more modern.

"*The Art of Keppy*," Uncle Davy said. "I think the writer would approve."

We'd eaten our eggs down to yellow smears. Uncle Davy still had his lime-green apron on. He dragged himself across the room again, got his own *Keppy* copy, came back to sit with me, and together we were turning pages, reading bits of things out loud, comparing notes, giving ourselves little quizzes.

"Four things you'll need if you're lost and stranded," Uncle Davy said.

"Water, a fire that won't go out, a windbreak, and a bed," I answered. "Too easy."

"Best bedding if you're betting on the trees," Uncle Davy said.

"Balsam, hemlock, spruce," I said. "And cedar, if you have to."

"You a speed-reader, Lizzie?"

"I get along."

"Don't get too smart," he said, "for your own britches."

"Nobody says 'britches,' Uncle Davy. Not anymore."

"Sad," Uncle Davy said. "Things used to be so interesting."

"You know what would be more interesting? *The Art of Keppy*, but with better pictures."

"Don't look a gift horse in the mouth."

I stared at Uncle Davy, who refused to laugh. "What does that even mean?"

"'No man out to looke a geuen hors in the mouth,'" he recited, from what I guessed was the twelfth-century version, but he said sixteenth and left it at that, because now Uncle Davy had flipped to the back of *Keppy* and was getting a little too excited about an acorn mush. "Edible!" he said, pointing to a page. I flipped. He read out loud:

The dough is cooked in two ways: first, by boiling it in water as we do corn-meal mush, the resulting porridge being not unlike yellow corn-meal mush in appearance and taste; it is sweet and wholesome, but rather insipid.

"Insipid," I said. "That sounds delicious."

He touched the basket on the table, raised an eyebrow.

"Don't even try it," I said. "Not when I'm your guest."

"All right," he said. "But doesn't all this make you hungry?"

"For bear meat?" I said. "For crayfish? For grasshoppers?" I was skipping around now too, deep in the heart of "Living off the Country." I was thinking of all the things I'd tell Mr. Genzler when I got back home, when I found him after school, doing cool, smoky things with Bunsen burners. I'd have quotes stored up in the back of my head. I'd give him one every time he doled one out, an even exchange, scientist to scientist, naturalist to learner:

One of the best natural baits for bass, when the water is clear, is that fierce-looking creature

called the hellgrammite, dobson, or grampus. This is the larva of a large winged insect, the horned corydalis.

"Horned corydalis!" Mr. Genzler would say. "Where on earth did you unearth that?"

"Seriously, Lizzie," Uncle Davy said again. "I'm still hungry. Are you?"

"If you insist," I said.

I decided on waffles. I told him not to bother himself; I had everything handled. I got the box from the freezer. I fired up the toaster. We melted ice-cream-scoop-size butter over the top. We poured a gallon of brown syrup on.

We ate then had a good long nap—Uncle Davy upstairs and me on the couch and the flutters of the outside world high and mighty.

When I woke up and looked outside, I saw that the stars were starting to pop. I just lay there on the couch and watched. Then I tiptoed across the floor and opened the door and set up camp on the stoop and imagined myself building a browse out of spruce, staying warm by a fire I'd built with gunpowder and a looking glass. The air was cool, the kind of mountain cool that happens at night, even in summer. The stars were putting on a show. I watched for a long time before Uncle Davy came along and sat down, easing down because of his hurt, because of his old age, he said. He had his hands on his knees, on the lime of his apron, which he'd never taken off. I had *The Art of Keppy* on my lap. I thought of those deer back in the woods and the smoke up in the clouds and my mom four hours down the road. I thought about Matias, who I'd be seeing soon. I thought about that big word, "choose."

"This is one very fine apron," Uncle Davy said.

"That is one very fine book," I said, and I meant it, and in that minute I was happy, and if you think books by dead people are just something to move with the furniture, to dust with a feather, to stack your plate of someday pie upon, you don't know this story yet.

Sitting there, looking up, I thought we'd gotten the worst behind us—that Mom was where she had to be, that we'd tamed the fire, that every part of the adventure going forward would be a happy one.

Victim impact.

6

BE CLEAR, THEY TOLD ME. BE ACCURATE. VALUE precision. But the truth is in development. The truth is slow. What happened first, what happened next, what the order is, and what the meaning is, and sometimes the memories are gone. Sometimes they blow in too fast and sometimes they knock me staggered, and look. Up there. Through the window in the roof.

There flies a firefly.

There flies another firefly.

I'm in charge.

The clock has tocked.

Time to call this session off.

7

I HEARD YOUR CAR DOOR SLAM. I HEARD THE
front door open. I heard your shoes rushing up the first
flight of worn-down steps and then coming up the second. I heard the rub of each leg of your jeans against
the other, and the flutter in your shirt, and now you
come in and you are sitting here and you are waiting.

Your hair full of the wet heat of August.

Your eyes full of something I can't tell.

I've been lying here all night watching the window in the roof, the blinky fireflies, the rising moon,
the dark parts. I've been lying here remembering—
thinking how to tell this story—and then the sun came
up and then I heard your door and now you are sitting
here, and here's what I've decided:

I'll keep talking.

It was the next day. The newest Day-Glo hung on
the brass owl of the coatrack. I was reading *Keppy*, waiting for Uncle Davy to finish something he had started.

There is the dash of the gipsy in every one of us who is worth his salt.

wrote Keppy.

I read the line again. I liked it. But then I remembered Mr. Genzler, and I thought of what he'd say, how he'd read the line if he were reading: "Every one of us who is worth *her* salt." Mr. Genzler, whose wife used to work for NASA, is pretty much a radical when it comes to "Girls are science-worthy."

My uncle filmed his TV show early on Tuesday mornings. He shopped at Timber on Wednesdays, wrote his syndicated columns on Thursdays, went to the library every Friday morning to computerize and send his stories—five miles down the road was the library. They had Internet service there that wasn't so spotty.

So this was Wednesday, a Timber day, and I was losing myself inside the *Keppy* pages, not smelling the smoke from yesterday's fire, telepathically sending my mom the *I love you* message until finally Uncle Davy announced that it was time for the Deviled Eggs Express.

I grabbed my stuff. We went.

Timber sits down the road beside a store called Herbalish. It sells tire chains, flexi-straws, magazines, and snacks. There are four leatherette stools and a split-oak bar in the back, and you don't have to wait for your eggs.

The Dart was a one-seat-across kind of car, no buckets. It had a perforated leather steering wheel, tape on the upholstery, the smell of cardboard and old newspapers, a mini Judy Garland hanging from the mirror, her red shoes sparkling in the sun. My uncle drove it sweet, with its windows down.

"Mountain air," Uncle Davy said as he drove. "Immaculate blessing."

I breathed in. I swallowed. I thought again of Mom at home, taking her first pill, swallowing down. Mom and the nuclear—I hated the thought; I shouldn't have read so much about it. *Short-term side effects of radioactive iodine treatment may include: neck tenderness and swelling, nausea and vomiting, swelling and tenderness of salivary glands, dry mouth, taste changes.*

I watched the mountain curves. I heard the trailer clatter. I sent Mom my thoughts. I kept my promise.

"Tell me," my uncle said, "a story."

I talked cafeteria food and recess, Field Day victories

and Kelly Gardner, who decorated her arm with fake tattoos. She pressed them on and washed them off. She was a walking, faded cartoon. I reported the names of Pennsylvania butterflies: the red-spotted purple admiral, the hackberry emperor, the common buckeye. Words I'd put in my bio book.

"Thinking of looking for specimens this summer," I said. "To add to the collection."

Wearing his fabulous shades, Uncle Davy nodded.

The earth rolled by. The trees to our left, the crinkled valley below, the moose-crossing signs. I stole a glance at Uncle Davy's driving hand, the big ring that he wore on his little finger.

We turned into the Timber and Herbalish strip. Two vehicles in the lot. Now three. The Dart. A Chevy. The Bullet 500 Fox that belonged to Luke, who'd inked his arms for real and had owned Timber since he bought it from his father.

The door chimes chimed. Luke scratched his ear and made a fuss. "Lizzie," he said, eyeing me up and down. "You've grown four inches. At least."

"Family inheritance," Uncle Davy said.

I tugged at my tick-fooling socks. There are some things you don't want in your blood.

Timber was dark inside, noisy with flies. We took our place on the leatherette stools, Uncle Davy and me, got three eggs each, extra paprika. We were on our second round of Sprites before Uncle Davy asked again about Mom. This is how estrangement works when there's one person stuck between two others. When the only way for two others to talk is to talk through someone else and when sometimes you make promises you know you're going to break.

"Probably waking up right about now," I said.

"What are the doctors saying, Lizzie?"

"Mom says she's going to be fine."

He let it sit. We polished off our Sprites, spun off our stools, picked up our bag of provisions. The bell rang. We drove back in silence.

That night Uncle Davy, wearing his Day-Glo lime apron over his perfectly pressed khakis with his tie stuck into his shirt, made us thick French toast. It was, to use his favorite word, divine. We ice-cream-scooped the butter on, we poured the syrup thick, we ate until we hurt. Then we listened to the cicada songs through the crescent-moon windows we'd left open, and then Uncle Davy started telling me his stories, about the miser who'd died and left an attic full of jewels, and about the kid who'd found an antique chamber pot, and about the girl at the TV studio having a pair of twins. Sometimes when he laughed, he covered his smile—that turn in his tooth made him self-conscious. Sometimes he forgot, and either way he was so handsome.

When he was finished talking, it was quiet.

"You can call your mom," he said. "If you'd like."

"Thinking she needs some rest," I said.

"You could take it outside."

"It's all right, Uncle Davy," I said. "I'll call her when it's right."

He put his hand with the big ring on my head, let it sit for a bit. Then he rubbed his bad knee and stood up and climbed the ladder to his loft, to his golds and raspberry fade. I heard the water run in the bathroom up there. I heard him call down to me, "Good night."

"Good night, Uncle D.," I said, and I felt the burn from the smell of that smoke in my eyes.

After that it was stillness, infinite stillness, except for the songs in the streams we couldn't see and the sound of Uncle Davy breathing and the rustlings in the houses in the far-off of the road.

The next day would be Thursday.

The next day would be Matias.

We'd planned the day for weeks by now. Rendez-vous by way of watercolors.

Matias?

He—

I guess. All right.

But I'm only telling you some things.

8

MATIAS BONDANZA. LIKE I STARTED TO SAY,
early on. Only child of two New York University profs,
living his summers in that whitewash of a house that
was built to look like the country they had come from.
Built to last, two years new.

The first time I saw him was the year before this
one at Herbalish. He was ordering a round of biscotti
after a cup of steamed milk. Unusual, like my uncle
said. Unusual, the way we liked it.

The second time was in the back of the four-door
Wrangler that his mother drove. His metal stool was
tied to the Wrangler's top. Its four legs were pointing
up. The whole thing looked like a silver bug that had
been flipped on its back.

The third time I saw him was at Timber. Up high on
one of those leatherette stools, which could make you
dizzy if you spun. He was halfway through his Deviled
Eggs Express. He had his watercolors with him and a

bright-white empty book and a little jar of water and a furry watercolor brush, and down at the foot of the leatherette was the step stool that I'd seen before, tied to the top of his Jeep.

He was painting. He had left his unfinished egg on his plate.

Uncle Davy sat on stool number one. I sat on stool number two. Stool number three was where Matias's mother had been, but she had walked away, was doing her provisions shopping, buying eggs. Asking for spelt flour and Tabasco sauce, nothing I'd ever seen at Timber. So there was space between me and this kid who was painting something fiercely, who didn't look up so he wouldn't lose his thought or maybe so he wouldn't have to say hello. Corner of my eye I could see him working, painting very green and very steep, like the painting itself was a painting of perspective.

"You like eggs?" I asked after I couldn't stand it.

He nodded. Didn't look up.

"You a fan of paprika?"

He shrugged.

"Is that a masterpiece you're working on?"

"Of course," he said. "What else?"

This accent that he put on the words. I liked it.

Uncle Davy was wearing his tortoiseshell shades and his pink Ralph Lauren shirt and his orange jeans and his shiny loafers. Uncle Davy was being his TV self.

"A little impromptu on the word 'masterpiece,'" Uncle Davy said, leaning over me, so as to direct his words to Matias. "As translated from the Dutch *meester-stuk*. As when a craftsman is transformed into a verified master. As when—"

"Really?" Matias said, not looking up, and I couldn't tell what kind of "really" he meant.

"Matias?" his mother called. Right then and just like that. "You almost finished with that egg?" Her words full of Spanish sounds and extra letters.

Matias looked up. He turned to see me—real. He wrinkled his brow and rolled his eyes, packed up his paints, his brush, his book—a napkin blotting the still-wet landscape. He left his egg where it was and lowered himself from the red leatherette to the shiny silver stool. From the stool he lowered himself to the floor. He walked toward me. One floor tile by the next floor tile. Slow.

"Matias Bondanza," he said, looking up.

"Lizzie," I told him, looking down.

"David D'Erasio," my uncle said. "But call me Uncle Davy."

"Uncle Davy," Matias said, reaching out to shake his hand. He had New York's whitest teeth. And the world's best smile.

I knew all at once: Matias and I would be friends. At Timber and at Herbalish. In the woods, by the stream, beneath the trees as tall as sky. Matias would be part of us.

That was the summer before this one.

One year ago from now.

A lifetime.

9

SUMMER FRIEND. YOU KNOW THAT KIND? LIKE:
You're at school, and there are these people you know,
the people of "wassup," "hey," "yo," "guess," and
you know them all right, they're friends enough, you
vote them into student council, you trade apples for
bananas, you partner up. School friends. That's one
thing.

And then there are the friends of summer. The
ones from the pool or the camp or the adventure.
Matias was my summer friend, but he wasn't only that.
He was my all-year-round friend thanks to the postcards that he'd send. One-of-a-kinders. Beautiful. Rare.
Watercolors painted on one side. My name and address
on the other. That mark he'd make: *MB*, inside a flourish of a circle.

More perfect than there are words for, and, like I
said, I'm good with words. Uncle Davy called those
watercolors first-class collectibles.

Finds.

"Why do we need words when we have pictures like these?" he would say. And he would mean it.

That one. There. See? Right here by my bed. It's a little bent, but I don't mind. That's Rockefeller Center all lit up for Christmas Eve, as brought to watercolor life by my friend Matias. A million points of light and a star somebody grabbed from the sky.

Facts that you could Wiki: Matias Bondanza was born in Santa Tecla, which is in El Salvador, a long way from here. Born the year of an earthquake that crashed the jungle from its cliff shelves, knocked the city to its knees, swallowed people and the sound of birds. Hundreds of people. Uncountable birds. Born that year. Check Wiki. Matias Bondanza. A kid born not just the year of the earthquake, but also that very same day.

You'd be shaken up too if you'd been born that way.

But maybe you wouldn't have what Matias has, which goes by the name of proportionate dwarfism. I looked that up too; Mr. Genzler helped. Proportionate dwarfism is a short-stature condition, often the result of a hormonal deficiency, or a pituitary gland problem, or maybe even stress, and I've always guessed, but

I wouldn't know for sure, that being born during an earthquake and a million aftershocks was probably a little stressful.

I asked Matias once. He doesn't remember.

You know how everyone who is your friend right now was a stranger to begin with? How everyone seems strange at first, and then (you'll defend this with your life) they are most clearly not? Matias was a stranger once, but pretty soon he wasn't. He was someone unusual until he was the most good-usual of all, and we were friends, that is my story, that is what you came to hear, that is what I'm telling. We were two kids in the six million acres where the houses were far apart and where the stores were Herbalish and Timber and where the roads were full of gravel and where there was this vending machine nobody used parked by the side of the road. We were four, five, six, seven times of coincidence until we made our plans. Breakfast at the schoolhouse. Hike to the woods. Put a line into the ponds. Sit there. Friends.

He was a painter and I wasn't. He was short and I was tall. We could do anything together. Wherever we were, we were him with his colors and me with my specimens. (Rocks. Feathers. Stilled butterflies, if

I could find them.) We were me in my sneakers and tick-fighter socks, and him with his silver stool, which he tied to his back like a backpack. He'd look up and I'd look down. We'd eat tomatoes from my uncle's garden like the tomatoes were fresh apples. He brought me Santa Tecla guac. He asked about the *meesterstuks*. We watched my uncle on TV—the two of us staring straight ahead and my uncle staring back, through the TV glass, in black and white and vintage.

"There's our uncle," we said.

"There he goes again."

Matias would sit on the mission chair and I'd sit on the trundle. Matias would paint and I would look for butterflies. No questions asked. Just stories. And then our first summer ended and Matias went back to Manhattan and I went back home to Mom, and then what we had were postcards—his paintings, my words; his hoping, my thinking. Then my mother got her news and it was summer again and time for the adventure. "Choose," my mother said, because the doctors had said that she needed quiet and because she could not bear to call my uncle herself and ask him for the favor, and because why would I not choose the place I loved best?

I would call my uncle. I would ask him.

Choose.

Everything, when you get to be thirteen, has complications to it.

Matias had his canes by now and not his stool. He'd sent a postcard with an SOS—"Meet me here." A painting of the stream, and beside the stream the esker, and beside the esker the glacial rock, and above the rock an arrow painted pink as the Ralph Lauren my uncle wore, and then, not the customary thing, a couple of watercolored words.

And then his mark: *MB.*

Thursday, after breakfast, after the Cream of Wheat made perfectly right in a brand-new pot, after the bowls were stacked in the cast-iron sink that still had a ring of black in it from the fire, I said, "Time for my rendezvous with Matias."

"You need a ride?" Uncle Davy asked.

"Nope."

"You've got it covered?"

I touched the postcard with the rock. I packed my backpack with my *Keppy* and my book of words and my pencil and an empty specimen box and also my headlamp, and a thermos full of melting cubes, and a bag of M&M'S, a box of granola bars, and a pocketknife, thanks to Uncle Davy. I hitched it on. I nodded.

"You tell Matias his uncle Davy says hello."

I tugged at my cap, roger-that style.

"You tell him . . ."

My uncle thought for a bit.

"That next time I see him, I'll find him a find. You make sure, all right? I'll have something waiting here for when he comes around."

I tugged at my socks. I opened the door. I went down the steps, across the drive, across the street, and up. Straight into the bio world of leaves and frogs and squish.

There are the rules of the six million acres. Landscapes and myths. There is what you should be on the lookout for, and there is what you'll never see, or maybe see but only once. The bear. The bobcat. The coyote. The fox. The wild turkeys that will snap at your hand, and the snakes that will sizz and the parts of the forest that will leave you with an itch if you have not read your *Keppy*, if you are not worth your salt, and also, there are rare birds out there, like the least bittern, which is a heron you can fit in the palm of your hand like a bunch of emergency facts if you are lucky enough to find one, if you are on guard, if you are a biologist, if you are brave. I always was.

Spoiler alert: I never found the least bittern.

10

SIX MILLION ACRES. SIX MILLION. THAT'S WIDE
and that's so far. I had my sneakers on and my socks
stretched to my knees, the perfumery of bug spray all
upon me. I had my *P* turned back on my head. I was
prepared. I had crossed the road and cut up beneath
the trees toward the nearest stream. I was moving my
hand like a windshield wiper to distract the no-see-ums
that weren't distracted by the spray. I was watching for
roots and looking up into the trees, which seemed like
sky because there was nothing I could see above them.
I had gone I don't know how far, but I wasn't lost, I
knew. Just find the stream and the gravelly ridge beside
the stream, then follow up. Keep going until you find
him.

"Meet me here," Matias had written. That whale of
the rock beside the best nook of stream.

And there, right there, he was.

High up on that rock that we liked the most because

it was shaped like a rock with stairs. High up with his two new canes, nicely polished and crossed. He was wearing the pink cap Uncle Davy had given him once, to make him a member of the family. His hair was a black gloss. Steam was rising from the stream and from a leather bag beside him, and on his lap, small as it seemed, was the book of paper and the tray of color and the squirrel-hair brush I'd given him last birthday.

He had heard me coming and he smiled.

"Hey."

"Hey."

You can't run fast with a backpack like my backpack on your back, but I hurried my Field Day best up the last part of the hill.

He wore a saint around his neck, a polo shirt, a pair of green-and-purple plaid madras shorts, and in the precise place that he was sitting it was like someone had turned a spotlight on. He didn't stand up. He smiled his piano-whites smile. I got real close, then stopped.

"Matias," I said.

He said, *"Pupusas."* With a dip of his chin.

National dish of the Salvadoran. *Masa de maíz. Chicharrón. Queso.* Cooked on a griddle in that white house down the road and carried out to the rock by the stream in a pouch that held steam, and there he was, where he said he'd be, and there I was. Both of us ten months older than we'd been, and both of us keeping our promise.

I stepped up to the rock and I climbed. Fit my sneaks into the rocky stairs, scurried to the flat top, plunked down beside Matias, plenty of room for us both. He'd crossed his canes into an X. He was making a watercolor, pretty and green. There was that superior smell of those *pupusas*.

"I knew you'd come," he said.

"Fast as I could."

High fives.

"I knew you'd be taller."

"I'm not that much taller."

"You are," he said. "I'm not."

"You're still cool as a mule," I said.

"Mules are cool?"

"Mules are stronger than horses," I said. "They're also more independent."

"Is that another Mr. Genzler fact?"

"It's our fact now," I said. "We own it."

He put the paints and the paper and the brush off to one side. He opened the pouch and unwrapped the foil. One *pupusa* for us each. A third one for us to share.

Middle of morning. In the woods.

You never ate such a dream.

The stream sang. The birds did. The bugs minded their own business. When the sun from far away broke through the sky of trees, the glitter on the big rock shone. On the stone beside us Matias's watercolor was drying in the air. He leaned back and closed his eyes.

It was the last week of June. Soon it'd be the first week of July.

"Ready for anything," I'd told my mom.

He was the world's best best friend, and the weather that day was so good.

11

SO YOU LEFT AND THEN YOU CAME BACK. SO THE stars came in by their ones and then went fizz, like someone had popped the top off a can of Mountain Dew. So you could say I slept, and when I slept, I dreamed, and now the morning has come in through the skylight, and we're past yellow, we're past pink, we're into the first blues of the day.

Wild blues.

And you're here.

It's our third day.

The daisies are still standing straight in their cup, the yellow melting the petals.

They have all the power to them.

Pupusas.

Right.

And Day-Glo.

I said it. I said "Matias." I said he was "the world's

best best friend." I meant every word. And now you are here and you want more, but I'm in charge. I will be getting to it. I'm just going to sit here. I'm going to sit here and be quiet.

12

ALL RIGHT.

Maybe.

I'll tell you something you already know. The parts of the story you're a part of.

Everybody called it Little Siberia. Little Siberia. The prison down the road. Little Siberia. Like it was a whole other country.

Everybody figured we were safe.

But that's not what you had figured.

You knew that something bad was starting.

You were out there. Waiting. You were, in fact, part of the bad.

I hate my father for many things. But I'm so glad he taught me courage.

13

THREE THOUSAND PRISONERS. FOURTEEN HUN-
dred guards. Thirty feet of concrete walls between
crimes and freedom.

It was miles away. It was summer. But it was no
other country.

This is what you came for, right? This is the heart
of your story?

Tell it fast, and tell it straight. Tell you what we
thought we knew. Tell you how it was.

That's what you want? That heals? That's what you
think?

Hear this:

The thing about history is that it's still ahead of us.
Every day, and the day after that: History is what we're
making.

See?

I lie here looking back and there is me with my
backpack and there is Matias with his *pupusas* and there

is our first day together in our second summer, and for all my words and all my thinking, I don't have describing power. What I want you to know is who Matias was—the stories he told with the roll of his *r*'s and the stories that came through the mail and the greens and the browns and the brights of his country.

His myths.

I want you to know who he was, because without that, nothing else here matters.

14

FOR EXAMPLE:

According to Matias in the stories he would tell, he would never have left his country, except for the gangs. He would never have gone away, except his parents said they had to, and he was nine, after all, and his country was hurting.

Gangs stopping people in their cars as they drove. Gangs yanking necklaces right off people's necks. Gangs scouting people out for kidnap. Gangs holding the coffee farms for ransom.

Once, Matias's mother swallowed her diamond ring so the gangs couldn't take it, and once, two men climbed up onto the red tiles of the roof of their house and through the bougainvillea and into the courtyard and then into the house and stole silver trays and silver-ware, certificates, Matias's jar of coins, and even with the guards he was not safe, even with the man with the machete who walked beside him to the school, to the market, walked as slow as Matias had to, on legs that couldn't go.

So Matias needed protection, and Tiburcio was his machete man. Tiburcio, who had spent four years in jail once on account of that machete. Tiburcio was not a part of any gang. Tiburcio was a kind and gentle man, a kind and gentle murderer. Tiburcio was Matias's best friend, his personal protection, but even then Matias was not safe, so the family left.

They packed, they drove, they flew away. The Bondanzas left their country.

That is their story, but so is this. There was beauty in El Salvador that no gang could ever take.

Black sand beaches.

Parakeets like flowers.

Waterfalls in jungles.

Butterflies the size of bats.

Moonlight like dew and daisies.

Going swimming naked.

The white blooms on the coffee trees in spring and the red beans at picking time, the beans rumbling inside the burlap coffee sacks.

The good and the hard. The bad and the missed. By the time Matias was ten, Manhattan was his city. By the time he was twelve, he owned a piece of the rock in a six-million-acre summer and remembered Santa Tecla with *pupusas*, and I was sitting beside him, his best friend, and Little Siberia was far away; it was not part of our story.

It wasn't from Matias that I first heard the words "proportionate dwarfism." It was not from Mr. Genzler. It was from my uncle Davy, the man who believed that difference makes us gorgeous. The man who taught me that for absolute fact.

If I don't tell you the before of what happened after, if I don't explain it all, *this* true, none of anything will matter.

So the time goes by. Tocks in the clock.

15

YEAH. I KNOW. THAT PART ABOUT TIBURCIO.
Murderer *and* heart of gold. Exactly what I said,
because it's possible.

Just not possible for everyone.

Just not always true.

You have to know the difference.

Tiburrrrrcio—you roll the *r*'s. You imagine that
whale of a rock with the *pupusas* steaming. Imagine
the stream that ran like a hook in a nose, that stream
that carried gold leaves on its back. Imagine Matias and
me, watching the stream and watching the bugs buzz
in, then slam against our protective perfumery. Imagine me imagining Matias, and remembering.

I wish I had the *r*'s to tell it.

I wish it were Matias telling.

If.

Tiburrrrrcio was born of the Pipiles, which is like
being born of a myth. Tiburcio had his own little

one-room house with its cool dirt floor and thatched-up roof in the coffee cliffs. He'd been a coffee picker in the hills and a gardener of birds in the city. He'd polished the silver for Matias's mother, cut the tangerines from the tree, helped the maid, her name was Nicha, on cleaning day. He was short and also strong. His skin was walnuts. He wore a braided hat on his head and a guitar on his back, and he was wearing that hat and that guitar but also his machete strung from a beaded sash and dipped into a leather pouch on the day of the murder that put him into jail for four long, wrong years. His machete with the polished tip. His machete, which he touched to the heart of the man who had hurt his daughter, bad; what choice did Tiburcio have?

There is such a thing as honor.

Once Matias asked me this and now I ask you: Can you imagine Tiburcio sitting in a Santa Tecla jail? Every single day Matias's mother visits. Sometimes she brings Nicha. Sometimes she brings Matias. Always she brings something for Tiburcio. *Yuca frita. Chiles rellenos.* Of course *pupusas.* Every day, for four years, she does this, until the judge shortens the sentence, or maybe Matias's mother convinces the judge, and does it really matter, because Tiburcio is free. Free to be Matias's best friend out in the open, to walk everywhere beside him like a shadow.

To the school. To the market. To the barber. To the club. Don't let anything happen to Matias.

That braided hat. That busted guitar. That machete in its leather holster with its beaded strap and leather pouch.

Can you imagine?

I bet you can imagine.

I imagined too.

I imagined like it was my own El Salvador.

Anything can happen, everything *has* happened, and this part goes before the next part, because if it doesn't, the rest of it won't matter, you will not be able to see, you will not be able to imagine the beginning to the end of it.

What happens is always mixed up with who it happens to. One thing is not alive, one thing cannot be fixed, without the other. What matters is the truth and how it's very complicated, how one story builds into another story. El Salvador isn't your country and Matias wasn't your friend, and we are here, in Pennsylvania, near New York, four hours and a couple of bumps away from what you think you want to know.

Are you sure you want to know?

Think about it.

Victim impact.

We are here, and far away gold leaves float on the stream and the least bittern is hiding and good people do bad and bad people do good and you have to forgive more or less within the lines of their intentions. You have to act according to your heart.

I can see the heat of right now through the window.

16

IT'S LEMONADE. WITH ORANGE SLICES.

I thought maybe you would want a glass of it too.

I thought a thousand things and I'm still thinking.

When is a secret not a secret?
When is telling a story stealing?
When is telling a story giving your own self away?
When is telling giving your friends away, your uncle, your mom?
How is any of this healing?

The ice in my glass cracks and cracks and now it's melting. An orange seed floats on my lemonade, like a ship on a sea of sugar.

17

THAT AFTERNOON I CAME BACK FROM THE ROCK full of stories. I told Uncle Davy everything new. About Matias and his *pupusas* and his New York City. About the trees and the streams and the birds.

"Lizzie." Uncle Davy came to me when I was sitting outside, after dinner on the stoop. I had *Keppy* on my lap, but I wasn't reading. "Call her. Please."

He handed me his old portable phone, size of a car battery (or almost). He went back up the steps. He closed the door. I dialed. I heard him crank Sinatra up on his old record player.

Privacy. Distance.

"Sweetie?"

"Mom."

"How are you?"

I told her how not anything had happened. No bobcat on the prowl. No sizz of snake. No scat of bear or even skunk. I told her about Matias and the rock and the steam, and she sighed. I told her about the over-dose of paprika on the Deviled Eggs Express, and how Uncle Davy had a new estate sale that was coming up—no secrets in that story, no busting estrangement rules. I didn't tell her about the fire and I didn't tell her about Uncle Davy's knee, but I told her how it was to sleep again on the trundle at night, and how I'd finally found a way to be so that the new four inches of my body fit. I told her I hoped I wouldn't grow any longer.

"Sweetie," she sighed. "Growth is in you. In your genes."

I shook my head. I mouthed "no," even though she couldn't see it.

I tried to imagine Mom while we were talking. Wondered if the tornado of her hair was still whirling, if the radioactive iodine was already streaming through her, if she was feeling the thick of it, the symptoms. I tried to think if she was lying down or sitting up, then I predicted lying down. I wanted to do something good for her. I opened up my *Keppy*.

There was still light enough to read by—light coming from the schoolhouse, light falling through the crescent-moon windows, light falling from the sky—so I flipped to the first page and read:

To many a city man there comes a time when the great town wearies him. He hates its sights and smells and clangor. Every duty is a task and every caller is a bore. There come visions of green fields and far-rolling hills, of tall forests and cool, swift-flowing streams. He yearns for the thrill of the chase, for the keen-eyed silent stalking; or, rod in hand, he would seek that mysterious pool where the father of all trout lurks for his lure.

"Oh," Mom said. I could hear her listening. I could hear Frank Sinatra behind me, Uncle Davy singing, and then, again, through the phone and all its wires, I could hear Mom lying there, imagined the medicine burning through, a war inside her skin. I could hear the distance between us and the distance between them, the rub of the bugs and the hoot of the owls that were getting ready for their midnight hunting. I could hear the starlight coming.

"Mom?"

"I'll take that to my dreams," she said, her voice growing paler and paler. "The green fields. The streams."

"Good enough," I said.

"Good," she whispered. "Very."

"'Goodnight moon,'" I said.

"'Goodnight stars,'" she said.

Like we'd always done, since the beginning of time, or the time that I've known through personal living. "Goodnight moon" and "Goodnight stars." Before Dad and his own disease were gone. When there were three of us in the house, but only two of us with love, when she hadn't had the courage yet to tell that man goodbye, when she and my uncle were the best of friends, when nothing had yet come between them.

Mom's voice was pale. There was nothing more. We said it, and I clicked off, and there was a split in the long distance, and when I came back inside, Uncle Davy turned Sinatra off. He waited for me to tell my mother's news, but I couldn't; what was the news, and hadn't we promised?

"How is she?" he said.

"Taking *Keppy* to her dreams," I said.

"That's good," he said. "That'll be a help."

He was waiting for more, but I couldn't say more.

Uncle Davy's eyes were brown and also green and I could see myself in them.

That was dusk. Then came the trundle and the night and the drift of all my thoughts toward my dreams until I was dreaming not of kettles or the trees or the Sinatra or the hoots of the owls, but of my father. I was dreaming the sharp edge of what he called his charisma, the bright flash of his personality, like the fifty-four thousand degrees of a lightning strike, the hard knock of everything he was and everything he wanted, and now in my dream it was my father who had poisoned my mother, made her weak, put the cancer in her. He lifted his finger. He touched her. She sizzed. I could see this in my dream because in my dream my mom wasn't just pale, she was transparent. She was touched hard and hurt by him, and the cells inside her scattered.

Narcissistic personality disorder. You already know what it is, so I'll say it: That was my father. He was like a clump of uranium, tossing off rays, and I am 50 percent him by the laws of science, but some laws are meant to be broken; that law I break each day. That night I waited for morning to come, and finally it did, finally it was all peace in the schoolhouse cabin, it was just me and my new four inches in the antique trundle bed, some bird and bug song beyond the window.

Uncle Davy was rattling around. He was putting on his green socks. Coming down the ladder. Calling.

"Lizzie?"

I didn't know, none of us knew, about the break at Little Siberia.

There are murderers with hearts of gold.

And then there are murderers. Strictly speaking.

There's what's in your genes and what's in your heart.

The blood of it.

I didn't know about the break.

But you did.

18

FACTS AS I HAVE READ OF THEM, AS THEY HAVE been reported in the news.

They were in the honor block. They had plans the size of Hollywood. They had decided in winter that by summer they'd be free. Fireflies and rippling breezes. Peanut butter and marshmallows. The songs of kettles. Fishing.

Through the wall of one cell, behind the cot where one slept, they hacksawed a hole. Through the crawl of that hole they found a kingdom. Of pipes and wires, steam and catwalks, catacombs and tunnels. They walked around for months at night. They measured out the miles. They had a set of clothes for their prison life and a set for walking in the kingdom. From one side of one tunnel to the long side of another they could see the air beyond, the little town, the acres of trees and owl hoot and abandoned lodges coming. They could see the old railroad trail that cut straight up through it. They could see the mountain ledge.

They'd walk around, then crawl back in. They waited until summer came before they broke for freedom.

You know how when there's a storm or Earth event, they show you TV maps that have some beating in them? Like, here's the epicenter and here's the pulse and here are the red circles spreading? In the days after the break from Little Siberia there were maps like that, which I didn't see until lots of long weeks later. There were maps and indications, sore spots, trouble zones, and in every map from that time now gone, the schoolhouse cabin was part of the story. There it stood, thirty miles west of Little Siberia, with its purple door and its crescent-moon windows, its tomatoes slowly blooming, its '69 Dart and its trailer. There it stood, and across the road and up by the stream, balanced on the esker, was a rock the size of a small Gibraltar, with little cracks in it where feet could fit, a rock with its own built-in ladder.

"Lizzie?"

My uncle Davy called, while thirty miles away at Little Siberia two straw-stuffed dummies were fast asleep on the cots of two escaping murderers, and there was the sound of something leaving inside the pipes and all those tunnels, and two people out walking their dog thought they saw two men pop the top off a manhole and wave their hands hello.

Must be two sewer workers, the dog walkers thought, though there wasn't something just right to it.

Must be.

And there they went, the two men running, in their tailored prison best—down the hill, through the town, past the post office and past the deli, to the edge of the trees, turning around one last time and yelling, "Sayonara."

"You up?"

I was already up. I was stirring the pot. I had the Cream of Wheat going and my pack fat with survival tools and snacks and *Keppy*. At the table, on the cloth, beside the basket of polished acorns, were all the Polaroids and the green note cards that Uncle Davy had piled there the day before, his writing day.

He had a bow tie at his neck. The strings of his apron tied loose at his back. He lifted the record player needle and put Sinatra on. Then he sat down and I brought the cream, the sugar, the raisins, the Cream of Wheat cooked to perfection.

"Meesterstuk," he said.

He pulled his glasses from his head. He sorted pictures.

Friday. In the groove.

19

THE THING ABOUT COLLECTIBLES IS THAT YOU can put a name to them, a guesstimate of value. Mint condition is what you're going for. And when you find it, how you find it.

My uncle's favorite era was Victorian. Victorian with its interiors like miniature museums. Victorian with its beautiful and amusing objects from all around the world. Uncle Davy talked Victorian on his own cable show, and on the shows where he was interviewed and to the estate-sale crowd, even to Luke at Timber, who is inked from tip to tip and dyes his mustache but not his ear hairs. Miniature. Beautiful. Amusing. The Uncle Davy words.

On that table were his Polaroids, and beside the Polaroids were his note cards, and on the note cards were my uncle's most extremely cursive words. My uncle's letters wore big hats. *Q* loops the size of tidal waves. *T*s the girth of a cross. *S*s like fishhooks. My uncle's letters were an art unto themselves. And then there were the words.

Hope is the thing. Hope and remembering.

Cursive that comes in close enough:

Gentlemen never ventured out of the house before first applying their Macassar hair oil during the 1800s. But then what to do about those terrible greasy stains that soon appeared on every parlor chair? Trust the resourceful lady of the house to solve this perplexing dilemma by knitting antimacassars—handmade pieces to protect the furniture from nasty stains. Three-Piece Crocheted Armchair Set: $88.

It was a Friday. See? The sun streaming through the crescent moons, a touch of the edibles on our Cream of Wheat, Frank Sinatra singing "Ac-cent-tchu-ate the Positive," which, if you haven't heard it already, pretty much sounds like you'd expect. Uncle Davy was matching the note cards to the pictures, double-cross-checking the facts. He was putting his one hand up toward his face whenever he laughed, and he was making me laugh and then he was laughing even harder,

God's elastic earth trembling beneath us, until all of a sudden he stopped, put down his spoon, straightened his loose bow tie, and said:

"Lizzie. You have to tell me. How is your mom?"

The thing about people who aren't much talking to each other is that they have to find a way to talk the love that still flows through. Most of the time, no matter what, people want to manage through.

I told Uncle Davy about the previous evening's long distance. I told him the stories I'd told my mom. I tried to remember something actual and direct Mom had said, some kind of news, some progress or some story she had told me that would not, in my retelling, break the promise I had made, and then I realized that it was me who'd done all the talking, right up to "Goodnight moon" and "Goodnight stars."

"How is your mom?" Uncle Davy asked, and I sat there, very quiet.

He watched me. He waited. I lifted my shoulders up. I dropped them. I thought about Mom's voice—pale and far away. Thought about my dream, call it a nightmare. Thought maybe it hadn't been a right thing, me coming when Mom was so sick, maybe I should have insisted on staying, maybe she really wanted me to, maybe there would have been a way, despite the doctor's orders: "Radioactive iodine can make other people sick." Maybe Mom really meant, when she said "Choose," that I should choose to stay with her.

Maybe the doctors were wrong.

"She's okay," I finally said.

Uncle Davy shuffled his Polaroids and note cards into a sloppy deck. He stacked the bowls and took them to the sink. He collected the raisins and the sugar, then crossed the floor, climbed the loft ladder, walked around up there, quiet as a cat. After a while he came down again, and all that time I sat. The taste of the morning on my tongue.

"Let me show you something," he said, walking toward the trundle. I crossed the room. I sat beside him. Frank Sinatra had stopped singing under the force of the needle.

In his hands he carried a long rectangular box. Its lid was a checkerboard—regular squares against varnished ones. The embossing read, "bloomingdale's." Some of the lid corners had been yellow-taped into ninety degrees, and when Uncle Davy slipped the lid from the box, the room whished with the sound of paper crinkle. A smell of old rose up.

He peeled away the paper. Inside were sepias and pinks and blues, newspaper stories, passports, important stuff, all of it punched through in places, ripped. There were scratches through the jackets, blobs in backgrounds, buckled edges, crookedness, places where the color of the picture had worn off, and if you were to ask me, and since I'm telling you anyhow, I'd say it all had the look of having been torn down in a hurry. Once on a corkboard. Now in a box. Broken, bruised, and split apart. This was it. This was then. Collectibles, but no mint condition.

My uncle had the celebrity touch. He made one palm flat. His palm became the past.

"August 1965," he said, gliding his palm with the picture closer so I could see. "The boardwalk."

I saw a tall boy in a plaid shirt and light shorts past his knees. I saw a girl beside the boy wearing a wide side part and three buttons on her dress. Behind them was a tall woman and a shorter man, old-fashioned, wearing their Sunday best.

Two sets of two. Four sets of history. Collectibles inside a photograph. You couldn't see their feet, but they were coming for you. You couldn't hear a word they said, but you knew. There was a girl. And there was her brother. Mint condition.

"I was ten," Uncle Davy said. "And she was four."

He stacked another picture on top of that picture, and now the girl had long, dark curls and a cap on her head and my uncle was beside her in a white suit and a tie so red you could see it in the photograph. His hand was up beside his mouth. He was covering a laugh. Her head was not even as tall as his shoulder. There was a certificate in her hands.

"Army gave me leave," he said. "She graduated first. Top of her class."

He sat and I sat and time ticked. No one was singing but the birds and the bugs that went *buzz* and then, sometimes, against the crescent moons, *splat*. With his free hand Uncle Davy rustled in the box again, found what he wanted, and stacked that picture up on top—a woman and, beside her, a man, and between them a baby with one foot tiptoe prancing on each of their laps.

"The coronation of you," he said.

I looked like a puppet, hung from some strings. I had one finger in each one of their hands. I was the smallest thing you could imagine, couldn't imagine being small as that, and then Uncle Davy dug some more and changed the view and now it was me playing pots and pans, and my mom above me on a ladder, her jeans full of splatter, a paint can like a bracelet hung down from one wrist, a smile the size of a river running cutting from one ear to the other.

"See that?" he said.

I did.

"Miniature. Beautiful. Amusing. The M-B-As. Whatever it is that you're not telling me, your mom will be okay."

I said nothing.

"If you want to tell me."

I shook my head.

"Okay," he said. "Fair enough."

I couldn't hear the stream or the frogs or the fish. I couldn't hear Matias up on that rock, with his two canes crisscrossed beside him. I couldn't hear him, but he had to be there, he would always be there, that was our plan. Directly after Cream of Wheat, rain or sun, come to our whale of a rock. There he'd be, upon that throne, keeping his *pupusas* steaming.

Out on the road there was a car or two, but they

came and they whooshed and they passed.

Uncle Davy tucked the tissue paper back in, closed the box, pressed the yellow tape back up against the corners, slipped the box into the shade beneath the trundle. He went to the sink and the dishes. He left me sitting there, thinking.

I leaned down.

I lifted the lid off the box.

I unpeeled the tissue paper. Quiet.

I found the picture of my mother and her brother, ten years old and four years old, united. I pressed it to my palm. I opened my *Keppy*, stuck the picture inside, slid the *Keppy* into my pack, that picture being a mint-condition story for me to tell Matias, a story about where I'd come from to set beside the stories of where he'd come from; stories are for trading. A girl and a brother traded for butterflies as big as bats. A sister and a brother, united, traded for Tiburcio and the roll of *r*'s. I slid the lid back on the box, slid the box back into the shadows, put my hands onto my lap, and left them there. When my uncle turned and looked back, it was like nothing else had happened.

Nothing stolen yet besides that photograph.

It was a Friday. Newspaper column filing day. Uncle

Davy finished his work, removed his apron, tied his tie, grabbed his keys off the brass hook.

"You want to come with?" he said.

"I'm good."

"You going out with Matias?"

"I am."

"Tell him hello from his uncle," he said, and he blew me a kiss and I blew him one back, and I called out so that he could hear me.

"To the M-B-As," I said.

"The M-B-As." He tipped an invisible hat.

Five minutes later he was headed down the road in his '69 Dodge Dart, dragging the trailer behind him.

20

PEOPLE ASK ME, WERE YOU AFRAID?

You asked me.

And I say, when? What part?

People say, did you have a hunch? And I say, explain to me a hunch.

Sun through the moons. Birds in the trees. Bugs in their riot. I could hear the bits of the road tingling the belly of that car.

And then I heard nothing. Quiet.

21

SOMETIMES YOUR EYES DRIFT TO THE SKYLIGHT above me, that rectangle of sky. You can't see the clouds that are gone. You can't see the clouds that are coming. You can't see the storm in the distance. But there is that rectangle and inside that rectangle is my portion of the sky, and you sit there, and you see that, and I am watching.

It's two o'clock in this afternoon, and there's no going back on this now.

The bad thing has started.

My uncle was gone.

I was off to see Matias.

I need *you* to see Matias, before he slips away, before the rest of this gets told.

You close your eyes. You know it's true. I keep reminding you: You have to know the person before you know the plot.

You have to know him *more*.

22

PROPORTIONATE DWARFISM IS A MISUNDER-
standing that begins in a pea of a gland.

The pituitary, the master. It sits inside a hollow place back behind the bridge of the nose. In the basement of the brain.

You can't see it.

You can't touch it.

It sits. In charge of some things.

Matias. Was something. Matias. Had those bright-light eyes, that black-fringe hair, that forehead *this* big, like a storage chest for his thoughts. He had hands that knew how to turn color into pictures. He had *pupusas* representing for his country, a beautiful country, despite the dangerous parts, an M-B-A of highest ranking. Matias had Tiburcio and those cool rolled *r*'s. He had ideas about who people really are. Matias had that stream, it will always be his stream, and he had that rock, and he could climb it. He had two canes, just temporary canes, thanks to an operation he'd had for reasons I'm not sure of. He had that stool he sometimes carried. He had that white house in the woods that I said we called the snow fort, right over the stream, to the west of the rock. He had my uncle as his uncle and me as his good, best summer friend, one head and a pair of shoulders taller. He had proportionate dwarfism, which is just two words, and you know this, right?

Nobody is the judgment they've been given.

Nobody's the label, the T-shirt, the slogan. Nobody's the category or the entry in the manual of diagnoses. Nobody is anything except who they are.

23

THOSE TWO PRISON GUYS HAD PLANS. THEY had a getaway car, parked at the ridge. Not a great car, not a good one, just a beat-up Honda nothing even close to mint condition, and filled up with the goods they'd need, and by the time they walked, then ran, themselves up to the ridge by way of the abandoned railroad tracks, by the time they found the key in the ignition, by the time they blew the car out of its park, by the time the till started to do its business on the metal auto belly—by then the Hollywood part about the getaway car was losing all its limelight. They'd planned on Canada. They got as far as two miles in the direction of west, and the car bailed out, it was done. The car wasn't going any farther, and they had to choose. What to carry. What to leave. To push the car into quick hiding or to set the thing on fire.

Two men on the run.

Two men all over the news. CNN specials.

Two men who'd need some ransom money to get them up to Canada. Two men who thought ransom was a kind of working plan.

I was setting out—tick-outsmarting socks to the knees, *P* on my cap with the bill to the back, my backpack crammed with everything I'd need, plus *Keppy*, plus the photograph, plus the emergency facts I'd transferred to the inside cover of the book before they vanished altogether off my sweating palms. Emergency facts being not much more than the numbers I was to call if there was a phone.

Uncle Davy would be back by two. I'd be back by some time after that to make the pie we'd make with the rhubarb he'd buy. I'd meet Matias by the stream up on the whale of that rock, and I'd look for the stills of butterflies for my specimen box, and he'd paint, and we'd talk. I'd show him the *Keppy*. I'd show him the two—the brother and the sister, hand in hand, united—and he'd tell me more about El Salvador, then something, maybe, about the private school in Manhattan and the subways he took and the underground elevators that carried him in and out of the dark parts of the city; he knew all the elevators. He knew the secrets of what he called his vertical distance.

I locked the door. Looked both ways at the road. Nothing was coming. I crossed and climbed up into the path between trees. The old logging path had been padded down by a fox, or maybe a bear, or by my uncle in the fall and winter and spring, when I wasn't around to walk the six million acres for him.

"You've got them covered?" he'd say to me.

"Covered."

The earth is many layers of itself. Sometimes a stone will come out of the dirt or the dirt will be the dust of trees or there'll be so much damp moss that you have to reach for a low limb so you don't start slipping back. There were all kinds of places in those woods that could lead to being lost, but if you found the near stream and kept to it, if you stepped across the fallen limbs instead of trekking all around them, if you walked across the backs of rocks and up the stairs of living tree roots, you'd find your way.

You'd see the same saggy squirrel nests in the crooks of bur oaks and black willows. You'd see the similar spiderwebs in the staghorn sumacs and nannyberries, the same I LOVE YOUs in the skin of the hop hornbeams. As big as six million acres were, you could take them small—one stream at a time, the dribble of eskers, trees with personalities, landmarks to sight for, until, finally, the big whale of the rock up past the hook in the nose of the creek came into view.

I was singing "Ac-cent-tchu-ate" and sometimes clapping my hands, which is what you should do to keep the bobcats and the bears away. I passed a landmark hut, one of those shelters left behind for anyone needing some survival. I reached the Y in the trail and heard the rattle of a downy woodpecker banging for bugs. The path pushed up at a harder angle. I shifted the pack on my back and still climbed, past the mass of dwarf dogwoods and the bilberry, past the hollow rock where once, last summer, I'd seen the timber rattlesnake, like a black garden hose, coiled up in the shade.

From the snow-fort house to the big-whale rock was maybe ten minutes walking east—over the stream by way of two planks that Matias's father had put there for him. The way from the schoolhouse was maybe thirty minutes north and steep. My sneaks were up to it. My bug spray was working. I was twenty minutes in. I was twenty-five. I was where I could see the rock, and I saw the rock—the silver legs of the stool flipped like a stranded bug, the limelight shine of the sun.

"Matias?" I called.

"Matias?"

His name echoing out across the six million acres of earth.

24

SOMETIMES STORIES SAVE US. SOMETIMES THEY are the only stuff we have of the what-happened-when. Sometimes, even Mr. Genzler would have to admit, if I were talking to him and not to you, if I weren't in this predicament, if you hadn't let this happen, if I were outside right now, beneath the sky, running free on my own two unfractured legs, it's not the sciency list of facts that matters most but the feelings on the edges.

The memories and the rememberings.

Take, for example, my uncle Davy's loon stories. Loon. Yes. The bird. With the shadow of his puppet fingers, at night, he'd tell the loon tales. How the loon sleeps in the lake (a curl of one finger). How the loon dives through lake silence (no fingers at all). How one loon lives for another loon, one pair per lake (his finger touching his thumb to form a lake). How in March, in the cold air of Cape May, Uncle Davy and Mom would wait for the migrating loons at the Point, and the loons would come—floating backward in neat, dark seams, he said. The loons facing the current and sucking their feathers in to dive and dreaming about the summer on their Adirondack lakes.

My uncle's loon stories.

And then my uncle's *one* loon story—the one he told me only once, when I was twelve, the summer before this one, on the last night of my first summer adventure, the official estrangement just getting its start. "I was twenty-three," my uncle said. "I came to the mountains for my first time. I came with a friend. We rented a cabin by a lake."

My uncle, who wasn't famous yet.

"It was June," my uncle said. "He cooked the dinners. I baked the pies. No one but us and a pair of loons, and every night on the cabin porch we sat, listening to their love songs.

"A loon can laugh," Uncle Davy said. "Did you know that?"

A loon can giggle.

A loon is biology, but a loon's a phenom, too.

So they sat. My uncle and his friend, they sat. Best friend, my uncle said. Best two weeks. Ever. Two and two and a lake. All they needed. No one looking in on them. No one asking questions.

"What happened?"

I turned in the trundle as he told his tale. Followed the beam of light up to the loft. Saw the shadow of my uncle sitting there, on his gold-and-raspberry bed. His hair frizzed out. His TV powder off. His eyes looking dark inside the shadows and trusting me with his whole story.

"I lost him," he said. "One year later. To a hemorrhage. The blood rushed to his brain. It was our first anniversary. We had come back to the lake."

Outside we could hear the cicada orchestra. The sizz of snakes. The owls. Inside it was quiet except for the yellow light, which hummed.

"What was his name?" I asked.

"Greg," he said. "I bought the schoolhouse in the woods so that I could be near him again."

"Is he?" I asked. "Near?"

"I like to think he is," my uncle said. "I like to believe in his ongoingness."

Where are you? That's the call of the loon. That's the story my uncle told. That's the stuff outside the edges that's bigger than biology and proteins, no offense to the clan of kick-butt girl scientists that I will someday be a part of.

"Matias," I called. "Matias. Where are you?"

25

I DON'T REMEMBER IF I RAN, BUT MAYBE I DID. I don't remember how my heart felt, except for the squirm of it, like it was riding a carousel inside my chest.

There was something to know, but I didn't know it yet. Anything was possible. In that split of that second it was.

Matias down on the other side of the rock? No. Matias just a few steps west? Not even. Matias clapping off a bear? No. I heard no clapping.

"Matias?" I kept calling, and his stool was there and he was not and now I realized that something else was where Matias was not: the *pupusas*.

No canes, no cap, but the stool and the *pupusas*.

He wasn't anywhere nearby.

"Matias?"

I scrabbled up the rock, past a blot of spilled paint, but I didn't bother to look close. There was the empty leather sack, minus its *pupusas*. He wouldn't have brought them and eaten all three and left. That was not Matias.

"Matias?"

I stood on that rock, my hands to my face, and called. The trees and the bears and the bobs did not call back.

"Matias?"

My heart carouseled inside my chest.

People ask me, were you afraid?

What do they think?

What do *you* think?

I was out there in the woods alone.

Matias was gone.

The word is "terrified."

26

I HEAR THEM JUST OUTSIDE, CLOSE, THE PEOPLE who bring you here. The men. Two men. I hear their voices. Always watching the window. Always close. Always near, if I need them.

Soon there'll be the setting of the sun.

Soon there'll be the blue of the blue moon rising.

Soon you'll stand, the tallest thing in this room, and I'll lie here with my heart beating wrong inside my chest. The bad thing has started and, again, I'm terrified.

Your shoes going down two flights of steps.

The door opening.

The car driving—you in the backseat, the two men in front.

The blink of fireflies.

You're free and I'm not. Or that's how it seems.

27

THERE'S ONE PIECE OF GLASS BETWEEN THE SKY and me.

There's one big blue moon past that glass. That would be the extra moon, the second full moon in this month.

I wonder if you can see the moon, from wherever you are right now, on this night.

I wonder where they take you when you leave here.

You never say.

I never ask you.

This is my story.

It's called the betrayer moon. On the other side of the glass, it stays until it disappears. Now there are only stars in my slice of sky, and my thoughts are turning into dreams and my dreams are turning into regrets, and even if none of this is actually my fault, I feel like it is. I keep asking myself what might have happened if I'd left sooner on that Friday to meet Matias. If I'd climbed the forest hill faster. If I'd been more aware, paying better attention, doing the work of a real biologist. If I'd have heard the crack in the woods. The scream.

Time, time, time.

Whooooosh, whooooooooosh.

I can't stop the ifs.

I can't stop the pain.

My uncle was beautiful. My world was beautiful. The things we did were beautiful. The things I had, the summer before this: The Deviled Eggs Express at Timber. The breakfasts-for-dinner in the cabin. The way my uncle would put the Sinatra on and dance— wild beauty into motion. The way Matias and I would sit in the cabin watching Uncle Davy on his TV shows, Matias half watching, half painting. The way, afterward, when it would be getting close to dark, we'd pile into the '69 Dart and drive the couple of miles down the road and up the bend to the white house, with the trailer rattling behind us. We'd drive straight to the top and park, and Matias would climb out, grab his stool, take his pouch, and right about then his mother would open the front door, step out, wave hello, and that was all we'd ever see of Matias's mom, who had come to this country from El Salvador. That house like a secret.

"Good-bye, Matias," we'd say.

"See you tomorrow," we'd say.

"Don't forget the *pupusas*," I would say.

The summer before this, when I was already the queen of biology and already very brave, but not half queen or brave enough.

Afterward Uncle Davy and I would drive back, windows down, listening to the sound of the crickets and frogs. It'd be too pretty to go inside, so we'd sit out on the stoop, watching the sun fall through the trees, little grabs of yellow light, like fireflies. We'd talk about my uncle's latest finds, the antique gossip, the tea at Herbalish, the kids I knew at school, the most interesting facts about *Pinus* spp., which is the scientific name for pine trees.

Sometimes, some nights, Mom would call during her break at the Tin Bar, where she'd gotten a job being hostess. Uncle Davy would dig the phone out of his apron pocket and put it to my ear and leave me there so I could listen to her giving updates on the regulars. The old man who had a tattoo on one cheek who wore a snake at his neck—a thin yellow thing, she said, delicate as a chain. The young kid, skinny as a bean, who drank his Coke and rum from a square glass he brought in from home, a real vintage, she would say, because she wasn't sick yet, or she didn't know it yet, or she hadn't told me she was worried, and then it would be dark, and I'd go inside and lie back in my trundle bed and watch as, from up above in his loft, Uncle Davy would start to talk about the second-prettiest place on Earth: Cape May, New Jersey. He'd talk about September after the crowds had gone and the birds rushed in, and how there were dolphins in the waves. He'd talk about my mother and him, out on the beach, chasing the sand-pipers that ran around like they'd all just been let out of a prison.

"We were best friends," my uncle Davy would say.

They were.

Everything changes.

My slice of sky has brightened. The day is on. There will be the sponge bath soon, my breakfast on a tray, the questions: "How are you?" "Are you . . . ?" "Do you . . . ?"

After that I will hear you coming.

The slam of the door.

The men on the walk.

The rub of the legs of your jeans.

The sound of your shoes on the stairs.

The first flight of stairs and then the second, and by then the blue moon will have drifted so far past us and you will be the height I didn't expect, the prettiness, the way you sit, the sadness in you, because there is sadness in you, because you know just what you did.

Victim impact.

You will sit in that chair right there and I will talk and I will wonder if I will ever leave this place again.

28

WHERE WAS I?

I was calling for Matias.

I was calling.

He didn't answer.

"Terror" is a shorter word than "terrified." But "terror" feels more true.

29

STANDING UP ON THAT ROCK, I SAW NOTHING but trees and path and a stripe of sun and that stream. I hurried down the stony indents and circled the rock—around and around and it was hard to breathe, hard to know what to do, and the third time around I saw a pair of orange newts rushing out from beneath the shade.

Two orange newts, like roadside signs, rushing over the leaves, across the twigs, into the shadows, toward the old logging path, and there, ahead of them, I saw it. Matias's cane. Just one of them. Pointing farther east into the woods, away from the path, where the poison vines wrapped the trunks of trees like snakes.

I ran as fast as I could, the low limbs going *thwack* against my shins, the emergency numbers in *The Art of Keppy* forgotten for the minute and probably, already, useless, but I didn't know that yet, I didn't know anything except I was calling for Matias and Matias wouldn't answer and my heart was going *bang*.

The bugs were thick as paste. I half closed my eyes. It was harder and harder to breathe. And now the newts were gone and the squirrels above were going limb to limb in a frantic scurry like they knew, like they were trying to tell me something. I reached Matias's cane, just that one single cane, and picked it up by its curve, and that curve was warm, and the warmth was wet.

"Matias?"

He was somewhere out there. Somewhere near. He couldn't have walked that far that fast, and beneath the fallen twigs and the leaves were stones, cobbled granite, like walking a bony spine. Hard enough for me, too hard for Matias, and you can't know how it felt, how it is in the moment when you know something's very bad but you don't know what the bad is, you cannot name it, and you're spinning, and you need to be brave, you are brave, you try to remember your courage.

The way ahead was rocky. The width between the trees was running narrower and narrower, until any path forward would have to be crissed and crossed, in and out—no one straight pass, just the raw shape of the elastic earth, the way it had been intended and then dented by glaciers, seeds, and time.

"Choose," my mother had said.

Choose.

The bugs were paste. I closed my eyes. I could see Matias's face inside my mind. His eyes so bright. His forehead like a storage chest. *Think,* I thought, *what he'd have thought. Where he'd have gone, where he was running to or from.*

Running? Not with that body, still recovering fom surgery. Not with our pact: *Meet me at the rock.*

The *pupusa* pouch was on the rock. The flipped-up silver stool. The spilled paint but not the limelight of sun, because the morning had moved on, the sun was higher beyond the sky of trees. I could still have turned west. Found the newts, found the big whale rock, taken that pouch, that stool, and hiked not far up to the planked bridge, used my emergency numbers, my straight thinking, *Keppy.* I could have crossed the stream and run for help to the white house, but every second counted, and Matias was out there, and he needed me *now*; if I knew anything, that is what I knew. Somewhere east, north, or south of where I was, he was, and except for the birds and the squirrels and the fall of water, everything was silent.

30

THAT KIND OF SILENT.

Which is louder than a scream.

31

THE TREE LIMBS WERE LOW, THE GROUND WAS twisted, the direction was running in circles. If you aren't walking by a stream you already know or on a path you already love, it's easy to lose whatever smarts you have in the woods, biology or no biology, courage or not. I was fighting the paste of bugs and there was a hint of smoke and I should have stopped to wonder about that smoke, to ask myself: *What is this smoke, where does it come from?*

I didn't.

I didn't wonder until a long time after. Until it was much too late. Matias, I'm sorry.

I raised Matias's cane like a machete. I thought of Tiburcio, touch of the tip. I thought of how I'd protect myself if something happened, if I was in danger. Just a touch of the tip. If.

Meanwhile:

The bad men had left their car.

They were on foot.
They needed ransom.
But you know that.
You helped them.

32

THERE'S EVERYTHING I DIDN'T KNOW THEN
and everything that I've learned since, and then there's
what I remember, which goes from vivid to confused
to a dream no one should have.

You're asking. You're waiting. You're sitting there
with your chin in your hands, your body leaning forward, the core of the apple you just ate leaving a stain
on your jeans, and what I remember next is this:

A fox showed up with a raven in its mouth. A red
fox with two wings drooping like a fat mustache. You
ate your apple straight to the seeds and stem, and now
I'm watching the sky through the glass to help me
remember and what I see is the fox.

The eyes of the fox were ovals, gold in the sun.
The raven's coat was purple black. "Are you staying
or going?" I asked that fox. "Have you seen Matias?"
I stood there asking. I stood there pleading, and the
fox began to run, like it had seen or it did know, and

I followed it up and down, the tip of that tail, the sound of it vanishing off, and now there were less trees and more bushes—rhododendron groves— and it was dark inside the green, and I had to cane the leafy limbs off, had to thwack and thwack, but I couldn't keep up, and after a while there was no more fox, no more purple-black bird hanging down like a mustache.

Every second counted. I'd left the whale of the rock and the stream I didn't know how far back, and the fox was gone, the smell of smoke was gone. I heard a riot in the underbrush and thwacked. I heard nothing else except me walking forward now, the cane thwacking the bushes to one side, *thwack* and *thwack*, my feet barely keeping up, my heart pounding, and it was so dark in there, so full of snag and itch, and I kept going until at last I heard the sound of water falling.

The bushes thinned.

The trees rose tall.

I walked.

"Matias?" Calling his name still, looking for a sign still, my sneakers rubbing at my ankle bones, and I stopped. The water was falling from the rocks like two white teeth biting into a dark-green pond. A cool spray skimmed off the water as it dropped.

"Matias?"

I'd gone way too far, and I was lost.

33

BY MY FEET, AT THE EDGE OF THE POND, A TROOP of ants were carrying one slight twig on their backs. The ants marched in a single-purpose file, headed to I don't know what, maybe a hole in the ground, and it made me so sad, because all those ants had a plan and I had no plan and maybe, I thought, Matias had, in all this time, gone back to our rock. Maybe Matias was out there somewhere calling for *me*, worrying for *me*, needing the cane I had stolen from the ground.

"Matias?"

You know how big six million acres of park is, and how every tall tree can look the same, and every twitchy rhododendron and every criss and cross and every rock could be the tree, the bush, the cross, the rock, you walked past ten minutes before. You know how hard it is to keep a coolheaded count of the little hills and dips and the bugged-out bushes that you push through because a tree fell down over a path. I needed a major assist. I needed Uncle Davy and Matias's parents and a park ranger or three and a cop. I needed Matias, needed to know he was safe, needed to see him, needed a phone if I was going to make use of my just-remembered emergency numbers.

"Matias?!"

Too many acres and not enough signs, unless you count the newts and, after that, the fox.

I couldn't think of where my friend would be.

I couldn't think of why he'd gone.

"Ready for anything," I had said to Mom.

But that was a lie, and I'm so sorry.

I had to get back to the old schoolhouse, to Uncle Davy. I had to believe that he'd be driving up—soon?—in the '69 Dodge Dart.

That he would save us.

34

Panic.—In such predicament as this, a man is really in serious peril. The danger is not from the wilderness. . . . The man's danger is from himself.

35

KEPPY. IN MY PACK. I REMEMBERED AND UNZIPPED and pulled it out, brushed away my tears, plunked on a log, fingered past the useless bookmark, the photo of my uncle and my mother, young and happy, and read.

"The man's danger is from himself."

The girl's danger too, Keppy.

I skimmed the parts where Keppy was lost and couldn't tell north from south. The part where a first-class woodsman got mixed up in his own home hunting ground. The part where the man got lost in a patch of cane. I read to get to the point.

WHAT TO DO.—No matter where, or in what circumstances, you may be, the moment you realize that you have lost your bearings, there is just one thing for you to do: *STOP!* Then sit down.

I was ahead of him on that, sitting there on a mossy log, but I could do what he said next—take the tip of Matias's cane and draw a sign in the soft ground, mark my spot, my SOS to myself or to anyone else. Then I could take the tip of the cane and draw the path that I'd just walked, if I could remember how I'd walked. Sit very still, Keppy said. Remember how you've come.

Well. And. Maybe I couldn't do that?

How long have you been gone?

I tried to ask myself that.

What did you see that you'd notice again?

A fox, I thought. *With a bird like a mustache.*

What else? If you can't remember (Keppy said, I read), you have one choice.

Work yourself downstream until, at last, you find a road.

Downstream, I thought. *Down. Stream.*

There were two teeth of water falling and a dark-green pond. There was a trickle like a tear headed away from the pond, past my Keens and underneath that log and down over moss and rocks and tree roots. I turned and watched the trickle go and, thin as it was, for as far as I could see, it did not stop; it was a lasting silver thread.

Work yourself downstream, Keppy said.

I zippered him back into my backpack. I went as fast as I knew how, as I could go on my own—more afraid and bruised with thwack than I had ever been.

36

YOU SAW IT, YOU SAY. YOU SAW THE BLUE MOON, up there in the sky, free.

You saw it and you thought of me, lying here, beneath my rectangle of sky.

You saw it and you thought of how it might be if I'd been carried out of this room and down the stairs and out onto the lawn and been sat with. If I'd been laid out on the grass and watched the big moon rise and then fall through every blink of night. If I'd seen how maybe the moon wasn't truly blue, but rare, if some of my story weren't like the moon's story—not truly blue, but rare.

My story is blue, wild blue.

And it is rare.

You thought of me.

You thought me free.

It's coming close to noon. I can read the hour on

the clock. I can read the look in your eyes. I can tell that this is hurting you, but it hurts me more, I promise.

But.

Tell me more about the blue moon?

Because I can't tell you any more of this story than I just have, not right now, and besides, the apple seeds on your jeans are crying.

37

MY FATHER WAS A COMPLICATED MAN. MY father was someone whose nose looked like mine and whose ears bent like mine, and who could be so funny, he could be hysterical, he could make you laugh if you weren't crying. He could find you just the right thing and give it at just the right time—like green gumdrops, for example, or blue sneakers, or an Almost skateboard. He could give you a lot and then he could take it away, and I stopped knowing how to trust him.

A story about my father?

Well. Yes. Sure. There are stories about my father. You want one? Here's one. Very specific.

I was younger than now. My father had a new job, another new job—he was always losing jobs. This job, though, was going to be it; this job was going to last. He'd been invited to a convention. He took me and my mom, who was wearing her hair as a platinum blonde. "This is my wife," my father said in the hotel halls when he was introducing her. "My wife," as if all she'd ever done was marry him, as if she didn't have a proper name, and I wanted her to mind, but she wouldn't. She wanted to believe in this fresh start. She thought that was her job.

If I tell you about my dad, I have to tell you about my mom.

There were ten hotel stories, three wings, and one hotel pool in the center of it all. On the first morning of us being there, my father took me to the pool to swim. Woke me up, handed me my suit, told me I was coming. I didn't want to. We walked down the red halls in our towels and suits, went through the lobby and out the pool door, and there was nobody but us out there, with the sun just coming up and the water the temperature of melting ice cubes. Nobody else. Who would?

I sat by the edge of the pool wearing the towel like a cape, my dipped-in toes turning blue. He sat on one of those armchair rafts with the cup of coffee he'd made in the hotel room and the paper they'd slipped under the door and the gold chain he liked to wear over the tan he always worked on.

"Come on, Lizzie," he said. "Get in."

"Too cold," I told him.

"Don't be ungracious."

"I can't," I said. "It's too cold."

But my dad, who was more beautiful than maybe I've said, my dad, who could give and take away, had to be the star of this show. He wanted me to thank him for this thing I didn't want; I wanted to be asleep in bed. "All this trouble," he said, "that I take to find this job, to bring you here, to put you and your mother up at this convention, and you're talking about temperature. Be a little brave, Lizzie. Be a little *appreciative*. Get on in the pool."

I looked up at all those hotel windows circling the pool. I looked for Mom, but I didn't see her. I didn't know what choice I had, seven years old, daughter of a dad who demanded "appreciative." It was a new job, a fresh start. Get in.

"Come on, Lizzie," he said again. He'd floated his armchair raft down to the pool's deep end, where the first of the sun had come in. He was wearing his black trunks and his look-at-me pose—lying out like he was a movie star and not a sales associate for a hardware chain, which is what he was, my mother told me later, a full year later, when we finally talked of it. He wanted to be seen, to be looked out on by the conventioneers. Newest sales associate. Devoted father. Six-pack abs. Gold chain. Look at him. I was part of the story he had spun. There was no "choose." Come on.

I left the towel by the edge of the pool. I walked to the steps on the shallow side, where the shadows were, and eased myself in. Ankle to knee to hip to waist, my skin turning blue. There were cold little bubbles popping through my yellow-flower bathing suit, goose bumps on my skin. From his armchair raft in the sun, he waved me deeper in. Father and daughter for a morning swim. What a dad he was. What a specimen.

The floor of the pool sloped down and down and I walked it, bouncing high on my toes, hating every inch, wishing he hadn't gotten this stupid job, with this stupid convention, and this pool nobody wanted in the morning, not like this. I held my chin above the surface of the ice-cold water, and then again he waved me in, and right there, right like that, the floor of the pool slipped away and the deep end began, and I was dropped into the nothing of it, and I was too cold to swim.

I watched my hair pulling away from my head, the red polish on my toes kicking, my arms doing wild things. I watched me sinking, going down, flipping upside down. I opened my mouth to scream. Chlorine rushed in. My feet were up above me, ten red toes in a frantic kick.

I woke up on the hard ledge of the pool. My towel was soaked beneath my head. My mother, in a bathrobe, was holding my hand. My throat was full of the chlorine choke. My hair was everywhere. There was a second bathrobe, on top of me, a terry-cloth blanket keeping me warm. Far away, on the other side of the pool, I could see the blur of my father at the center of a small crowd—guests in their pajamas or their half-buttoned shirts, hotel men, security. I could hear his voice and his hero story, about how he'd rescued the daughter who'd insisted on a morning swim.

"You do what you must do," he said.

I couldn't talk for all the choke inside my throat. I couldn't say what was true, there on the ground; my mother was holding my hand. Out in the pool the armchair raft floated, the mug of hotel-room coffee, the newspaper, the sun.

"I rescued her," my father said.

But I knew it was Mom who had looked down from her hotel window. I knew it was Mom who'd run. Mom who'd saved me. Mom.

We were better off without my dad.

I knew that then.

But you: You believed in your father when you shouldn't have. You believed in him, and that's why everything that happened to Matias and Uncle Davy and me happened.

38

WHEN YOU'RE RUNNING THROUGH THE WOODS,
the woods are running you.

That's how it seems, since you asked.

That's how it feels.

You're blur and the woods are blur, and when the
brown suede moves and then the strike is white, you
realize it's a deer out there, maybe a stag, and maybe
you've scared it. Either that or it's on your team, clearing
the way through the brush, helping you downstream.

I followed the silver thread.

I followed the deer as it ran.

I heard my own feet and my own breath and the
pack thumping my back, maybe the squirrels overhead.
A mountain going down doesn't always go straight
down. The silver thread of a stream can disappear, hide
underground, and then it's back again, and the deer
is still running, just ahead, and you're running, fast as
you can.

I don't know how long it took, but Keppy was right. Downstream. It gets you there.

I could see the road, at last, from where I was. A flash of lights. I could hear "Copy that," "Stand by," "En route," and I kept running, knowing now that they'd come for us, that they'd heard my SOS, my cry for help in the woods. "I'm here!" I called, and the trees were thinning, and the asphalt curve of the road was right up ahead, and the edge of the mountain was tumbling, and I knew where I was, somewhere near Herbalish, six curves from the reno'ed schoolhouse. "I need help out here!" I cried, my words hoarse inside my breath, and now the crackle and the sirens answered back:

"Let me see your hands."

The trees stopped. The road began. There were four of them—state troopers—with their guns pointed straight at me.

I couldn't stop. I tried to stop. The speed was in me still, inside my Keens, raw and ripped, inside my ankles, twitchy.

"Freeze!" they said.

I put my hands up to my head.

"I can't find him," I said, out of breath. "I can't."

There were four of them, like I said. One woman and three men in gray wool shirts and black striped pants, Stetsons on their heads. There were two police cars, white as the waterfall, parked perpendicular to the way the road ran, lights flashing, and now the woman lowered her gun and approached, talked into her lapel. "We have," she said, "a minor."

"Stand by," a policeman said.

"Go ahead," said the female officer.

"He's not there," I said.

She walked first and the others followed. She said her name was Sergeant Williams, from Troop G. She had a purple band and a leather strap around her Stetson, patches on her sleeves, a thick black belt, blue eyes, and I was trying to catch my breath, and she came closer and closer, holstered her gun, kneeled down.

"Tell us your name, young lady," she said.

I said what it was. Lizzie.

"Tell us your address."

"The reno'ed schoolhouse," I said.

"Now slow down and take a breath," she said. "And tell us what you saw."

What I saw? I thought. *What part?* The paint, the steam of the *pupusas*, the newts, the cane on the ground—I still had that cane in my hand—and then the water falling, and the pond, and the silver thread, and the deer.

"He wouldn't have gone off," I said. "Like that."

"Who?" Sergeant Williams said, lifting her lapel microphone to her mouth, on the ready to report whatever I said. "Which one?"

"Which one?" I said. "Only one," I said. "Matias."

"He told you his name was Matias?"

Her forehead crinkled over her light-blue eyes. Her mouth frowned.

"Because his name *is* Matias," I said. "Matias Bondanza. My friend."

She stared at me. Shook her head. Pulled her lapel up to her lips, had the two-way radio on.

"Your friend," she said.

"Yes," I said. "Matias Bondanza." I was still breathing hard. The flashing lights were hurting my head. "He's not so tall," I said. "This is his cane," I said. "He left the rock. And I couldn't find him."

"You've been out looking for your friend?"

"Yes," I said. "Just like I said."

"A boy your age?"

"This tall." I showed her with my hand.

"We've got a possible kidnapping," Sergeant Williams said. Into the radio on her lapel. Into the crackle. To the three other men.

"What's going on?" I finally said.

"Affirmative," the crackle said.

39

YOU KNOW WHAT THEY DID. YOU KNOW ALL OF that. Put me in the back of a car with its lights swirly and asked me, over and again. Describe Matias, describe my path, describe what I saw, give what I remember, tell them the timing on that. It was Sergeant Williams, First Sergeant Williams, she said, the same woman with the blue eyes in the back of the Crown, writing it down. Every now and then some news would come in through the crackle, or some news would go out through the radio on her lapel, and I don't know how long it took, but it was soon by the time they had Matias's mom on the phone, and "affirmative that."

He'd gone out in the morning.

He had not come back.

Just like I had said.

"Received," Sergeant Williams said into her mike, and now she looked at me, steady, while Sergeant

Charles Rose pursued my uncle's whereabouts, called the cabin first, nothing, called the library, but he'd left, called Herbalish and Timber and the two friends whose names I had, but he appeared to be in transit; that's what Sergeant Rose, talking to Sergeant Williams, said.

"He's famous," I said.

Sergeant Williams pushed the bangs out of my eyes.

She shook her head.

"We're working on it," she said.

She asked me did my arm hurt, and I looked down. For the first time I saw the places where the thorns had dug in, the start of a poison-ivy rash on my elbow, a bruise already turning the color of a dark sky.

She got out, clicked the trunk, and returned. "Give me that," she said, meaning my arm. She was careful as she swabbed the alcohol on, fixed the Band-Aids, put the calamine on the open rash, the sick pink smell of it. She told me, as she worked, about herself. She had a kid named Sammy. Her husband drove a forklift truck. They lived beside a kettle pond, where the fish were best. She asked me was I hungry and suddenly I was, and now she was peeling the banana that would have been her lunch, offering some Cadbury chocolate. Left over from Easter, she said.

"What else, Lizzie?" she said.

My arm stung. The Band-Aid crinkled. I had banana breath. My ankles twitched. I looked past the first sergeant, through the car window, toward the other troopers, two of them hiking up into the woods now, Charles Rose standing by with his radio on.

"I still don't understand," I said.

Because she hadn't told me. Not yet. It was like she couldn't tell me until I'd given everything I had, and I had, or thought I had, and even then, due process of law or whatever it was, she couldn't fully tell.

"I thought you'd come for Matias," I said.

"We're looking for him now," she said.

"Who were you looking for originally, then?"

"The escapees," she said.

I didn't follow. I had the upside-down umbrella of the banana on my lap, the backpack still on my back, Matias's cane resting on the floor of the car.

"There's been a break," she said.

"Break?"

"At Little Siberia."

I looked at her. I shook my head.

"Two convicts," she said. "Armed and dangerous. We're following any lead."

I closed my eyes.

"Matias is out there," I said.

"We've got troopers, rangers, feds," she said.

She didn't say "I promise."

40

IT'S FAST AND IT'S SLOW, WHAT HAPPENED NEXT. I remember rushing underneath the swirl of light, up the curves of the road, past Herbalish, to the schoolhouse, the first sergeant driving and the staff sergeant up in the passenger seat beside her and everything crackling.

Then we were at the schoolhouse, on the pebble drive, pulling in behind my uncle's '69 Dart and his trailer. I watched the front door, waiting for him to run out—his green socks, his apron on. I watched the windows for his shadow. The only thing that I actually saw was the dust the car had churned up.

I started to climb out. Sergeant Williams called me back. Reached her hand around. Said, "Stop."

"This is my uncle's house," I said.

"Secure the property," she said to Sergeant Rose, but he was already out, walking with a hunch. He circled past the trailer and the Dart, past the bushes, to the back. A few minutes passed, and there he was, on the other side.

"Clear," he said, and Sergeant Williams loosened up, got out, asked me for the key, told me to stay put for my own good, to duck if anything happened, "Please trust us, Lizzie." She walked in a crouch. She joined Sergeant Rose up on the porch, and my heart sank because I knew that if Uncle Davy were okay, if he were home, if he were near, he'd be beside me now. He'd have come and flung open the door to the car and hugged me hard like that.

He would have known, looking at me, that I'd lost Matias.

Because that's how it was feeling by then. That I had lost Matias. That I hadn't been there, on alert, when he'd needed me. I had two strong legs and smarts and science, and I should have been there, I should have known, that's what you do for friends. You're *there*. You feel something, hear something, sense something, and you go running, and I didn't go running soon enough, and when I did, I got all tangled up in the woods.

Armed and dangerous. Cops everywhere. Matias missing and my uncle gone, and this was bad like you don't know bad, like nothing can prepare you for, like you don't know what to do with the banging drum of your heart, like you can't really breathe but you have to.

"Choose," my mother had said.

But I didn't choose this.

41

PLEASE.

Ask them for water. Call down the steps. Tell them I am choking, I can't swallow, I can't breathe.

I was afraid, okay? I was.

I was afraid, and that's not brave. That's not who I thought I was.

42

SERGEANT ROSE WORKED THE LOCK. HE CALLED my uncle's name, Sergeant Williams at his back. When Sergeant Rose turned the knob and pushed the door, they both stood back to a boom of silence—nothing and no one in there but the M-B-As. The loft above. The trundle below. The finds. The record player from which no Sinatra was singing out.

From the car I watched the sergeants, moving slow, then moving fast. Through the house, around the things, past the chalkboard, near the crazy grandfather clock. After I don't know how long, Sergeant Williams bent down and picked something up. Stood up. Read it out loud.

I had rolled my window down.

Dear Lizzie,
Danger is afoot. I've gone looking for you

If you return before I do, ask for help. Get to Matías's house.

"Second possible kidnapping," Sergeant Rose said. His voice going out through the crackle.

43

THEY ASKED ME TO PACK. THEY DROVE ME down the road to the snow-white house, where the police cars were parked at the top of the drive—the lights on, the sirens silenced. They asked me who else needed to know my whereabouts, and I thought quick and lied. What they didn't know they didn't know, and they didn't know my mother or radioactive iodine. They didn't know the healing that she needed. They didn't know the promise I kept. If they called, they would find my mother's secret out. Worse, my mom would find out about this.

I couldn't let it get to that.

~~Your mother needs quiet.~~

Secrets are secrets.

They're kept.

All this time, in all my knowing of Matias, I'd never been inside his house. It had always been its own country up there, its own white fort and castle. We'd meet at the rock, we'd meet at the schoolhouse, we'd meet at Timber and at Herbalish, but never here, not this sacred, from-another-country house, where Matias slept, where the *pupusas* were made, where we only ever dropped him off, and now I was standing there, and I'll tell you because you're asking me that this is what it was:

A square house with a center square cut out. Tiles the color of terra-cotta. Walls pure stucco white. There were silk parakeets hanging from strings and photographs of jungle cliffs and a collection of pinned butterflies hung from the ceilings or hooked on the walls. Between the house itself and the center court-yard there were four sides of glass, one door on each side, so that you could walk room by room through the inside, then open a door into a glass courtyard. Like entering a greenhouse. They were out in the courtyard when I arrived. Mr. and Mrs. Bondanza. Two troopers. Photographs on a garden table, like a tablecloth.

"Oh," Mrs. Bondanza said when she saw me. "Lizzie." Half standing, half reaching for me. *Come here. Come now.* I hurried through the glass door into the smell of gardenias and forced lilacs. I let her crush me with her hug. I slipped the backpack to the floor, fixed the cap on my head, gave her the cane I had found.

"He'll be asking for that back," I said.

Like waterfalls. Her tears like that.

"If," she said.

44

IF MATIAS CAME BACK.

If the convicts called for ransom.

If any man on the loose from Little Siberia approached.

If my uncle.

All ifs.

After a while most of the police people left.

45

SERGEANT ROSE DIDN'T.

He was on the lookout for a change in direction.

He was on the prowl.

From wherever I looked I could see him—the swoop of his belly in his gray dress shirt, the black stripes of his pants, the Stetson he never took from his head. He kept his radio on. He let the news crackle in. Sometimes I saw him in doubles. The real him and the reflected one. The wait in him. The watching. Wherever I was. Wherever he went. We walked in circles.

Not knowing is tragic. We were full of nothing known.

The hours ticked.

Come home. Come home. Come home.

We'd left my uncle a note. We'd called his phone. Sergeant Williams had found and taken my phone, saying, "We need to be the first line of communication." She stood with me and watched the windows with me and the doors for any sign. A newt. A fox. A cane. A boy. My uncle with his nephew.

Please come.

Nothing came.

So here I was now, at this snow-fort house with a garden stuck inside. Where Matias lived in the summertime, and where I'd never been before, because some people have secrets and Matias's secret was his house, the way he lived, at least part of him lived, like he was still in El Salvador.

The clouds had started to push out the sun. There was itch beneath the peel of the calamine, a stinging like bees along my arm, ache in my ankles. My head was hot inside the heat of my cap, and inside all that glass of that house I would sometimes catch a glimpse of me—the dirt still on my cheeks, the twisted *P*, the droop of my socks, the squints of my worry. I don't know what time it was when Mr. B. left the courtyard for the living room and sat down on the striped couch. When he reached for his iPad. Finger-tapped in.

I watched him. Through the windows. Through the glass. I came near. Stood behind him. He opened to an alphabet of Adirondack maps. Topographs. Aerials. Maps that went zoom. Six million acres of elastic. I stood watching as he found the snow-fort house, the schoolhouse house, the stream, the whale of that rock. He tapped, zoomed in, zoomed out, and then he asked me: "Re-create." "Re-create," with the rolling *r*'s. *"Por favor."*

Put the facts of my morning on the map.

I leaned across his shoulder and drew the whole thing out. The newts. The cane. The fox. The mess of rhododendrons. The patch where I got lost. The teeth of water falling. The same facts I'd told the sergeants. The same ground I'd covered, again, at this house. Everyone asking and me telling, and no matter how I told it, I had not found Matias.

"You're sure?"

There, or somewhere near there, I pointed again, was the fox.

There, or close.

Sergeant Rose was watching me work, standing at my side behind the couch. Mrs. B. had stopped pacing, had sat beside Mr. B. She looked up to find my eyes. Sergeant Rose looked back. They asked me to show them again, the same story, again, and now, this time, I remembered something I had somehow forgotten— that smell of smoke in the breeze.

"Be clear," Sergeant Rose said.

"Smoke," I said. "Cigarette smoke. Somewhere around here." I pointed. Then drew a circle out. I couldn't remember precisely. I wasn't really sure.

"I got lost," I said.

"You didn't mention smoke in the interview," Sergeant Rose said.

"I didn't remember." It was dry inside my throat, my mouth.

"We asked you several times to remember all you could."

"I'm just remembering it now."

"What else are you remembering?" He was standing beside me. His arms were crossed. He rocked back on his heels. Gave me a long, hard look, like I was the criminal here.

"Cigarette smoke," I said. "Just"—I showed the size of a puff—"this much."

He dropped the knot of his arms and pinched his lapel. He put his radio on alert. He rubbed at his head and tilted his Stetson. He smelled of a full day's work.

"This is a critical detail," he said, and now Mrs. B. was crying again and Mr. B. was rubbing her back with one hand, zooming the map with his other, trying to see the smoke that I said I thought I'd smelled. Had I smelled it? Yes. I had. I was pretty sure I had.

"I was looking for Matias," I said. "Not two men on a break." I could hear the tears in my voice. The guilt. How had I forgotten? Every detail counts.

"Smoke," the sergeant said. "Just a puff. Somewhere around here." He pointed. He asked me again.

Be precise.

Tell the truth.

The truth is a trick.

"Somewhere," I said, and nodded. "Yes." Closing my eyes. Trying to remember. Where in the woods I was. How the smoke had moved. Downwind from where? Could smoke ever blow up?

"Anything else we should know," Sergeant Rose said, "before calling it in?"

"Right here." I pointed. "There was smoke. Right here, or thereabouts."

Mrs. B. pushed her black hair back behind her. It had curled from the heat in the house. She stuffed a fist into the pocket of her jeans, tugged at her orange camisole, turned around again to look at me, because I was standing there, behind them, on the other side of the couch, on the other side of the world; that's how it felt. Her eyes were like two wells I could have fallen into. I was inside her eyes, and I was drowning, like I had drowned before.

"They have him," she said. "They have him. What else?" Her voice like a murmur. Like a rustle of birds. Accents and ruffles and hurt.

"Let's avoid summary conclusions," the sergeant said.

He touched his hand to her shoulder. Gave me a look. Called it in.

There was commotion through the crackle.

46

OUTSIDE, THE CLOUDS REPLACED THE SUN. THE
day grew dark. I throbbed. I stood at the front door of
the B.'s white house, watching the street for the Dart.
For my uncle. And his nephew.

Come home. Come home. Come back.

I had forgotten the puff of smoke. I'd been there—
eyewitness—and I'd lost a clue that could have mattered. A whole afternoon gone by and now night had
come on, and I'd been there where the smoke was, I'd
been close, and I'd forgotten, and maybe, I thought,
Matias had seen me walk by. Heard me calling his
name. Tried to call back but was stopped. I tried to
imagine how that would feel. I tried, and I got sick with
it. Choked up.

See me. Help me. Hear me.

I'd walked past.

Matias?!

My uncle with his slippery celebrity shoes was out

in the woods. Matias was out there too. I was in the snow-fort house, at the door, watching for lights on the road—the Dart, a Crown, something. I was there, just standing there, waiting. Nothing. Waiting is nothing.

Now, in the glass, I saw Mrs. B. behind me, her curls spilled out around her head, her fist in the pocket of her jeans. Watching the road, watching me, waiting like I was until I turned. She opened her arms. She hugged me close. She wasn't tall for a mom. I was taller.

"You are my one boy's best friend," she said with extra syllables.

I nodded.

"I know that you are doing what you can."

I sobbed.

I hugged her back.

We stayed like that for a long time, and then we turned.

Standing there. Watching the road.

Waiting is the worst kind of nothing.

47

MAYBE IT WAS TEN O'CLOCK WHEN SERGEANT Williams came back. Her cop lights on, her siren off. I heard her come up the drive and park. I ran and opened the door, let her in, called out for Mr. and Mrs. B., who were still in the living room, watching the news. I'd been watching too. Breaking news, CNN kept saying, but it was the same endless loop. Pictures of the escapees. Pictures of the car they'd left. An accomplice jailer in handcuffs, already accused. An inside job, they kept saying. Tools hidden inside food.

Now, behind me, CNN was showing pictures from the afternoon—the fan of troopers, the manhole cover, the possible escape routes, the topographics of six million acres. There was talk about police sources and challenges, pictures inside the walls of Little Siberia. CNN would be showing pictures of Uncle Davy and Matias soon. Uncle Davy in one of his celebrity shots.

Matias in one of the pictures they had sorted in the courtyard.

Both of them with the same word running like a river down below: MISSING.

They'd be showing them soon. They already had.

But now Sergeant Williams had come, and Sergeant Rose was at attention, relaying the nothing-new-from-out-there news to Mr. and Mrs. B., and leaving me with the first sergeant. There was a smudge of eyeliner under each of her eyes, no more blush on her cheeks. She was off duty, and she had a kid and husband at home, but here she was. More waiting. More regrets. I should have remembered the smoke. She was going to tell me.

"I know," I said. "I'm sorry."

She worried her lips. She scratched the skin on her neck. "Lizzie," she said, and I knew it was bad, whatever was coming. She led me back down the hall, closer to the front door. A private conversation. My stomach hurt.

"We've heard from your mother," she finally said, when we'd reached the door, when going any farther would have meant going outside beneath the sky that was dark with night and clouds. "She's very concerned."

Oh, I thought. *Oh. No.*

I nodded. I tried to picture my mom at home, her blood all smogged up with the medicine, her hair white at its roots. She was at home in the dark watching CNN. Seeing her brother on the news. My friend Matias. Calling my phone. A sergeant answered.

I felt full of the ugly then. All I'd done was wait. And forget a detail. And try—there was a promise—to protect my mom. Worst promise keeping I'd ever done.

"You said that there was no one else to contact," Sergeant Williams said. "We believed you. Under other circumstances we would have investigated, but Lizzie, we have a break on our hands. And two possible kidnaps."

Is there anyone else we should contact?

I'd said no. Shaken my head. Left my mother out of the mess we all were in, left her secret to herself. I'd had a plan. To find Uncle Davy and Matias first and then call Mom—get us all three on the phone, tell her the adventure we'd had. *See? We're okay. See? Nothing to worry about, Mom.* I'd had a plan not to tell my mother until the only thing to tell her was, *We're fine.* And she'd be so happy after that, and the happy would stand beside the hope she had to have to beat the cancer, and she'd get better like she had to, no interruptions. That would have been the story I'd tell. That would have been it, if my uncle and Matias had been found. If there weren't six million acres and two men.

And the person who had helped them.

Put their tools inside that food.

Sergeant Williams dug into her pocket, found my phone, tapped the screen. She crossed her arms and tipped back in her boots, like Sergeant Rose, and waited for the call to ring through.

"Mom?" I said.

She burst into tears.

"Mom. I'm sorry. I'm so . . . I thought . . ."

"Oh," she said. "Honey. What's happening there?"

But she already knew. She'd been watching CNN, like I said. She had called my phone and the sergeant had answered, and I had to tell her what I knew of the truth. That Uncle Davy had been filing at the library. That I'd gone up into the woods. That Matias was lost and his cane had been dropped and that I'd walked and looked, and I hadn't known. Not until I saw the cops had I known about Little Siberia. Not until we drove to Uncle Davy's house and found the Dart but not found him had I understood the horribleness of the trouble we were in. Uncle Davy must have heard about the break in the library or on the radio, I said. Uncle Davy was looking for me. Uncle Davy was that kind of—

"Yes," she said. "Yes. Lizzie. He is." And now my mom began to sob.

Estrangement or no estrangement, my mother loved my uncle, who was her brother first. It was my father's fault that they'd stopped talking. My father, to blame for this.

Sergeant Williams rubbed the liner from beneath her eye, looked past me, through the door, into the night. Because my uncle was no good out in the woods. He had never been. He had chosen the six million acres because a celebrity like him needed space. Because a man like him needed space too. Because he had lost something once. He walked the woods in slippery shoes. He never went far. He understood the trees and the bears and the glacial tucks through the books he'd read, the stories I had told him, the biology I knew, Matias's watercolor art.

"He has *The Art of Keppy*, Mom."

"Keppy?"

"*Camping and Woodcraft* like I'd read to you."

My mom on one side. My uncle on the other.

And now.

And now?

Sergeant Williams uncrossed her arms and scratched her head. She put her hand up on my shoulder. I listened to Mom sob and myself sob, and sometimes four hours and a bump and turn is much too far from the people you love.

"Mom?"

"Sweetie."

"We're going to find him."

"I love your uncle," my mother said.

"I know."

"I just haven't said so lately."

"He loves you back. He tells me . . . stories."

I thought of the photo in my backpack. The ways that families do begin and how they cannot end.

"He's being a hero, right now, Mom. Wait till you see. He's going to come home with Matias."

"I'm coming up there," Mom said.

"You had the medicine, Mom. You can't."

I checked the sergeant's face. She raised a brow.

My mom had not mentioned any sickness or medicine or doctor's rules to the sergeant. This much was clear enough.

"In a few days," my mom said, saying the words for hope's sake.

"In a few days we'll be all right. I promise."

Sergeant Williams motioned for the phone. I told my mom I loved her and gave it up. Sergeant Williams walked away, down the hall, opened a door into the courtyard, and they talked. Trooper to daughter's mother. Mom to mom.

I stood there, out of hearing.

Finally Sergeant Williams came back with the phone inside her pocket. She stood there, in the kitchen, beneath the hands of a clock. It was 10:26 at night. Sergeant Williams fixed the mess of her hair. Walked the circle of the house. Returned to where she had started. It was 10:31. She asked, "Who has eaten dinner here?"

Not one of us had.

"Mrs. B.," she called, and I heard Mrs. B. stand up.

"Teach me to make rice pudding," she said.

The weirdest thing she could have said.

Also the rightest one.

48

ONE FIREFLY. TWO. TWO LITTLE LIGHTS IN THE sky above the rectangle window that they sliced into the roof before, when my mom lay here, in this bed, waiting for a miracle. You have to see the sky to hope. The sky, because it is always new, always promising a future, because it's the only way I can forget, sometimes, the itch of the ivy in the itch of the plaster over every broken bone, the nexts of my story.

Tomorrow is day five.

Tomorrow, and the blue moon is past us now, and I'm counting.

You're counting, I can see it, too.

I wish to be outside. I wish.

Tragedy is fast and it's so slow.

Your shoes scuff the stairs on the way down.

49

BASMATI RICE. THREE CUPS OF MILK. ONE
cup of whipping cream. And sugar. And one half of
a whole vanilla bean. And water and a cinnamon
stick.

Mrs. B. had these things.

That's where I left this story yesterday, inside the
kitchen in the snow-fort house.

That's where we'll start again, now that you've
returned.

Mrs. B. showed Sergeant Williams how to salt and
simmer the rice, how to add the milk and cream and
sugar, how to knife out the seeds from the split vanilla
bean, how to fold the bean in.

She showed her that.

She showed her how to stir—not slow, not fast.

She showed her: "This is the way in my country,
which we left." The beautiful. The dangerous. The coffee and the coffee men. Tiburcio.

They cooked and they stirred and in the end they tossed the bean and all that time they were standing there, and sometimes Mrs. B. couldn't work for how panicked she was, jumping at every last noise outside, every new something on the TV or radios, and Sergeant Williams would put her hand on her shoulder and say something I couldn't hear, and she would stir again, taste again, keep going, and Mr. B. stood by, near, his iPad in hand, looking up and looking down, not saying anything, all his terror carried high and in his neck. I thought of all the worry they'd had in El Salvador. Of the reasons they'd come here, to my country. Of how they'd wanted safety for their son, how they'd come here for his protection, and now two men had climbed through the pipes of Little Siberia and pushed up out of a manhole and gotten a getaway car two miles in. Two men. And the B.'s son was missing. Not every murderer has a heart of gold.

It took forty minutes, maybe, of stir. It was way past Sergeant Williams's shift, and she had Sammy and her husband at home, but she was still with us.

"Oh," she said, putting a clean spoon into the pot. "That's good."

There was four servings' worth.

We stood there, suddenly starving, scraping our bowls clean.

Looking back now, telling this to you, I can see Sergeant Williams, with her bright-blue eyes and the black knot of her hair at the base of her neck. I can see her Stetson on the counter, hear her radio hardly crackly. I can see Mr. and Mrs. B. and how, after the bowls were empty, there was silence. Even the radio went quiet for a spell. You don't know how you are going to survive what surely plans to kill you, then someone makes rice pudding.

I could taste the good in it. And the fear.

Like Salvadoran Cream of Wheat.

50

THAT NIGHT I LAY AWAKE IN MATIAS'S ROOM. ON
the side of the house, one turn to the left from the
kitchen. I lay on his bed on top of his quilt with the
window open—hardly any stars out there, clouds over
the moon.

The paper parakeets hanging from ceiling strings
floated in the night breeze. An empty cage, like an
antique lamp, perched above my head. One wall of his
room was painted green, and three walls were painted
white, and above his headboard, pinned to the corkboard, were a bunch of photographs.

Pictures of Matias at a black-sand beach. Pictures
of Mr. B. inside a cove. A picture of Mrs. B. at the end
of a dock, unclipping a fish from a hook. A picture of a
swimming hole in a jungle cliff, Matias leaping, folded,
a regular naked-to-the-bone cannonball, the size of any
cannonball, no proportionate nothing. A picture of Mr.
B. drinking coconut milk from a hairy shell. Pictures of

a courtyard house, snow-white on the outside, a garden inside, flowers tumbling off the roof—purples and reds. A house like this one except it wasn't in New York.

But the best picture of all was Matias and the man with a machete hung from a beaded strap and tucked into a leather holster. The two of them walking toward the camera, their heads thrown back in a laugh. The man was taller than Matias, but only by a broken straw hat. His skin was dark as furniture polish.

As walnuts, Matias had said.

Tiburcio, I thought. *Tiburrrrrrcio.*

And there beneath the photographs, hung from a hook, was the machete itself, tucked into its holster. Right there, in my best friend's room.

Why would you keep a machete by your bed?

What was Matias afraid of?

Why didn't I know?

I turned the light off. I kept my eyes open. Through the window I heard the tymbal songs of the cicadas. Crepitations. A word my uncle had used one night last year when we were sitting on his stoop and he was telling me about his M-B-As and then he stopped.

"Listen to that," he said.

I listened.

"Every song has a purpose. The courting calls. The flick-flicks."

"Love songs," I said, and he said, "Crepitations," and I should have asked him then about love and about its opposite, which is loneliness. I should have asked him what he did without me, if he sang when I wasn't there, if he made his Cream of Wheat when it was only him at the table, if he ate his edibles, if it was always only him. I should have asked the man who loved me best, but there are some things you shouldn't ask, just some things you should fix.

If.

And now my uncle, my beautiful celebrity uncle, was out there, in the woods, with his slippery shoes, his pink shirt, his lime-green socks, his polka-dotted bow tie, his turtle-shell sunglasses, and I was thinking how loneliness is private and how fear is the loneliest thing of all, and he was out there because of me, but also because of Matias.

The night songs rushed and sizzed. Like someone shaking popcorn in an aluminum pan. The cicada songs would swell up and die down, and then the tymbals would play again, all these bugs calling, *Love me*, and it would go on, loud, then simmer off like a low-heat pot, then burble up again. I imagined the songs ricocheting over six million acres. I imagined Uncle Davy and Matias listening in. Wherever they were, they were hearing this.

They were alive; I had to be sure of that.

Alive and listening.

The cicadas were hissing. A sound like a dream, but I wasn't sleeping. I was remembering the last time my uncle drove the four hours west and south over the roads. The last time he'd come to visit. My mom had kicked my father out. She had finally had enough. She had been brave. That's what brave does. Brave protects others and brave protects yourself. Courage should be everybody's first and favorite hobby. Uncle Davy had come to help Mom rearrange all the emptiness my father'd left behind. He'd brought finds with him, an extra Dutch oven casserole, a grandfather clock, his Frank Sinatra records.

Accentuate. The positive.

"Listen to this, Sandy," he said. Sandy and Davy. Sister and brother. Back then, when they were still best friends. Sinatra was singing from the stereo my uncle had set up on the window ledge. Mom was wearing the yellow dress with the orange stripe up the zipper in the back. Uncle Davy was wearing his lime-green socks and his silk bow tie, a hint of pink to it. He was taller than she was, like he'd always been, and she'd dyed her hair an orange red, the color of a flame against her too-pale skin, like the sickness was already there, a masquerade trick. The living room had been mostly emptied out. I was watching through the stair posts.

Uncle Davy took a Charleston step, reached for my mother's hand. He danced his wild beauty. She didn't. She pressed a tea towel to her face instead, a chunk of ice to stop the swelling.

"It'll be better without him," Uncle Davy said.

"I know," she said. Her words muffled by the towel.

"You'll have your chance at happiness."

"I know," she said, and sniffed. "But still. It's just . . ." She looked around. He did.

On the steps I sat and stared. Thinking about my dad, the first-class narcissist. Gone. If you looked in a book about people with problems, you would find my dad, so much of a blow-up doll of an exaggerating man that you could put a pin in him and he'd pop. Narcissism is pretending you are what you aren't, thinking you're more than you are, putting a stomp over anything anyone else ever says, believing the dumb impossibles of your own made-up brand. Narcissism is *Look at me, I am.*

Narcissism is *You aren't.*

Narcissism is *I'll lie until I get just what I want.*

Narcissism is sometimes you're glittery, too, you're full of your charm, you're making promises anybody would hope you would keep, anybody would think you might keep, sometimes you keep them. So confusing.

I knew all the words. I'd grown up listening to them. I'd heard all the fights since I couldn't remember when. No job would have my father. Friends would come, but then they'd leave, they'd stay away. My mom had finally, finally said, "Go," but I didn't know, when she said that word, that I'd never hear from him again.

I didn't know that I wouldn't want to.

I didn't know how brave I could be. How, when you're a verifiable scientist, you can teach yourself to feel things.

What I knew was how suddenly empty our house

had become. Circles of dust where lamps had been. Stains on the wall where frames had hung. Fade in the carpet showing where the stuffed couch had been. A quiet you could hear beneath the Sinatra song. My father was gone and most of our things were gone too.

I was watching my uncle and my mom.

"He can't hurt you anymore," my uncle Davy said.

"I don't know what I'll do," Mom said.

Uncle Davy stopped trying to dance. He straightened his bow tie. He looked up at me and halfway smiled, covering his mouth when he did. Then he left the house, went out to the drive, opened the door to his Dart—I could see it all from where I sat—and came back with boxes of things, the M-B-As we'd fill the blankness with.

"Lizzie," he called to me. "How is your dusting arm?"

"Good," I said. "Enough."

"Do us the honors," he said. "Would you?"

So that's what we did. We dusted the circles. We rearranged the fade. My uncle filled the house with the things he'd found and restored and loved, the things that you see here in this three-story house of five little rooms.

My uncle had brought his things to our house so that our house wouldn't be empty.

And now he was lost in the woods.

51

I COULDN'T SLEEP. I COULDN'T KEEP MY EYES closed, there in Matias's bed, listening to the night, feeling the strength of the dark, remembering.

If they'd been found, we'd know. If there were a ransom wish, we'd have heard. If my uncle had made it back to the schoolhouse, he would have called or a trooper would have, or they would have driven up the road, come inside the white house, told us what they knew—more news, "you're safe," something. My phone was with Sergeant Williams, who was out in the courtyard, beneath the glass, watching for meteors, or sleeping. It hadn't rung. There was nothing to report on the radio crackle.

Time was passing, and I'd smelled smoke, and I'd forgotten, and it was up to me to find my way back to the tobacco puffs in the woods. To find the evidence, the start of a trail, the direction they had gone in. Up to me, or that's how it felt, say what you want, think it.

Retrospect is everything, but it was still the night—too dark to leave, to find my way back to the woods.

Too dark, but I had to do something.

I lay on top of that quilt. I thought of the photographs, the paper birds, the empty cage, the machete in its sleeve. I tried to picture Matias out there in the six million acres. Matias and my uncle. Short and tall. Young and not. Afraid and trying not to be. In the dark of the night, in the tweak and the twitter of the bugs and the birds so loud it probably hurt. Night sounds start in your ears. They go to your heart. They get stuck inside your bones.

They'd be hungry out there, if they were still alive. There'd be no sharing of whatever food the convicts had, or I could not imagine that. There'd be no lighting of fires to cook any fish or fowl they might have caught: too risky. My uncle and Matias were somehow there, they had to be there, with the convicts whose faces had been smeared across the news—their eyes like marbles in their heads, their hair combed back strict and unnatural, the stripes behind them in their prison photographs measuring how tall they'd stood on the nights of their arrests, years apart, for different crimes, one murderer no better than the next.

My uncle and Matias were there, out in the woods. They were hungry and cold. They had walked or they had climbed and they had swum or they'd been carried in their bow tie and their slick shoes and their bad hips and their one cane; I didn't know. The earth is dirt and moss and stones and sticks, and you need good boots, an Indian walk, first *Keppy* rule. You need equipment in the woods.

They needed equipment.

I could help them.

Couldn't I?

And didn't I have to?

The night was moving slow. I lay there with my eyes wide open, imagining, and then I was remembering and then I was caught inside the stories Matias had told about his El Salvador, the coffee farm in the jungle hills that his grandfather still worked. The trees made canopies, he said. The beans grew like clustered beads up and down the slender twigs. They started green. They ripened red. Christmas was the picking season, and there's a talent, Matias said, to pulling a bean from a tree. There's the sound of fingers picking, whole families out there, working the trees, stuffing their burlap bags, carrying from the low parts of the hill to the flat top, where Matias and his grandfather waited.

I lay there trying to imagine a different season, a different woods, the El Salvador Matias had loved and left for the first purpose of safety.

Each sack was weighed, he said. Each weight was put down in a book. Each picker was paid according to the weight of his sacks. Everything happening beneath birds and butterflies—green beans sorted from the red. Christmas. At the top of the hill Matias's grandfather weighed the bags and wrote the numbers beside the pickers' names inside his leather book. Matias counted out the cash from the previous week's work and paid. Tiburcio disappeared and then came back with a sack of mangoes on his back, the blade of his machete sticky with fresh juice.

This was El Salvador, Matias had said. His home. Until the gangs came and wanted ransom for the land, until they stood there with their guns and made their threats, and in the end the coffee trees were left.

Left.

Left for the safety of my country.

In the dark I waited for the dawn to come. I imagined Matias and my uncle waiting for the same dawn to come, all the songs of birds and bugs in their hearts and bones, all the not knowing of what would come next, and I had to come next, but there was still so much night outside the windows of the white house, and now I remembered another story Matias had told about El Cadejo, the white dog with the red eyes who protected faithful Salvadorans on the roads at night. The legend of El Cadejo. There was a good dog, a white one, and there was a black dog, devil owned, and both these dogs had bright-red eyes, and whenever the two dogs met on the roads at night, they went all out. Teeth and claws.

Worst fight you ever saw, Matias said—goodness against badness.

The sun was coming. The dawn. I sat up on that bed and watched the crack of light break through Matias's window and creep across the room, light things up from a slanted angle, put the paper birds on the move. The sun came up, and the machete hung and the cage was empty.

If I was going to put my courage into action, the time had finally come.

52

FEAR IS THE WORST LONELINESS THERE IS.

Also: thinking you're not doing what you can.

53

I FILLED MY PACK: *THE ART OF KEPPY*, M&M'S, three granola bars, water bottle, bug repellent, flashlight, that photograph of my uncle and my mom, the photograph I stole from the corkboard in Matias's room—the one right there, in the frame, by this bed. That's Matias in the hammock. That's the farm behind him. The jungle cliff. Tiburcio.

Like I said.

The air was insect song and the slant of the sun had lit the house and I borrowed two apples and borrowed some bread and borrowed three bananas and I had a plan.

What happened next was not the plan.

54

THE NIGHT BEFORE, SERGEANT WILLIAMS HAD washed my arm and reapplied the calamine. She'd left the bottle in the room; I reapplied. I checked beneath my Band-Aids, pulled my best jeans on, slapped down my cap with the *P* facing back, zippered the backpack. I had to move fast.

Be decisive.

Brave.

There was no one up in the white house. No coffee perking. No talking. Even the crackle of the radio had simmered to zero and the sergeant was asleep; I heard soft snoring. I whisked down the hall of glass and no one noticed. Down one hall, down the other, past the kitchen, to the front door. I hadn't put my sneakers on yet and my socks were quiet. I did not breathe until I reached the door. I turned the knob with the most extreme care and the lock retracted: slo-mo. I closed the door behind me.

Dawn. Or almost.

The pack on my back. The cap on my head. Tiburcio's machete strung across my chest. He'd touched the tip to the heart. That's all it had taken. It was morning, and I had my honor on.

From the front of the house I walked to the back. Through tall grass and the morning dew. There was nothing out there. No mulched fence. No beds. The Bondanzas' garden was in the middle of their house, a fortress of flowers protected, and everything beyond the house was grass leaking into wilderness, with a very gradual line between the tame parts and the wild. More grass than trees, then more trees than grass, and then I was in the woods.

The sun came in at a tilt. There was a soft path that Matias had worn into the earth with his canes. Over pine needles and tree roots, past toadstools, under nests, to the bridge.

The stream was low, needing rain. The bridge clattered as I walked. By now there was more sun in the woods—a fireball of orange in the distant faraway and a glow right at my feet.

At the whale of a rock I could see the boot scuff of yesterday's police. I could see where the dogs had pulled at their leashes, and where the troopers had stood and how the rock must have felt—exposed and guilty. I could see the ways the police had culled their evidence—the stool was gone, the quiet, the sack that had contained the *pupusa* steam. I fit my shoes in the notches of the rock and climbed.

There was a scramble at the base of the rock, and I looked down. It was those newts again, rushing toward the breaking sun, then rushing back into the shadows. I stood where I was, smelling the air, watching the fireball of sun in the far distance.

55

I CAN SEE HOW IT'S GETTING DARK AND HOW you'll have to leave and how the clock is ticking. How the sun's falling off and the sky is turning purple. The men who wait for you are jingling keys and talking. Sometimes I wonder if you tell them my stories at the end of our days, or if they drive you to wherever you go to in silence.

I don't know where you go.

I've never asked you.

It's evening here, but it's morning inside my story. It's morning and I am standing on that rock, and maybe tomorrow when you come back, you will tell me what the moon looks like from the windows you look through.

When you come back tomorrow, it will still be morning.

56

YOUR FEET WERE HEAVY ON THE STEPS JUST NOW.

You were walking slow, and now you're late.

Now you're here with a big yellow tote over your shoulder and a pair of sandals on, red toe polish, and I look up, away from you, toward the sky above my head, the clouds, while you settle in.

Who gave you the toe polish?

Who gave you the bag?

Why am I the one lying here? I didn't commit the crime.

You're late, and I didn't think you being late was allowed and besides:

I thought you wanted to know what happened.

Don't you?

57

I DON'T WANT TO SEE WHAT YOU HAVE BROUGHT me.

I just want to stick to the rules, which is I tell you the story in the order that I can, and then I ask you things when I want to. If.

You're supposed to listen.

You're supposed to pretend that you were me.

You're supposed to imagine what all of this felt like.

58

IN THE MORNING LIGHT, LOOKING DOWN AT that rock, I saw something I'd not seen the day before— the *MB*, inside the circle. The watercolor mark! Like Matias's own brilliant SOS, something he must have thought of when he saw the two men coming. Just one look, and he must have known, and so he left his mark.

For me to find.

"Matias," I said out loud.

Matias.

Like he could hear me.

I'd missed the smoke and I'd missed this and my eyes got hot with tears.

Go, I thought, I told myself. *No time for tears.*

The newts poked out of the shadows, scrambled east. The newts seemed to have a hunch, so I climbed down and I followed. My sneaks crunched the fallen leaves, scattered spiders, sent squirrels leaping. I scoured the woods, searching for something else that might have been left behind—a pebble trail, another mark, proof.

Please.

Wherever Matias was, that was where my uncle had to be. That's what my heart said. The two of them together. I had already decided and I decided again. Straightened the sling of the machete. Pulled the cap tight on my head. Yanked the sleeves of my flannel shirt. Slapped at the mosquitoes.

Followed the orange arrows of the newts.

Looked for other signs.

59

IT WAS ON THE LOW LIMB OF A TALL TREE THAT I saw the second scribble.

Near where the fox had been, on this side of the rhododendrons, where the oak had fallen and cracked into four big jigsaw pieces and grown a fur of moss, and this, I remembered, was where I'd smelled the smell, or somewhere close to here, of smoke.

But there was no smoke now.

I stood on the fallen oak to get more height. I breathed. Only mountain air, the smell of water sizzing, bird nests, fish, biology, but yesterday there'd been smoke and it had floated downhill, to somewhere like this. The smoke had come from up above. I'd smelled it and gone east and south, toward the two-toothed waterfall.

The ground was dry. No boot prints. No tip of a cane pressed into muck. But when I crouched low, I could see proof in the leaf rot, the ghosts of feet heading toward the higher ground, through the patch where the rhododendrons were worst, where walking through would be like trying to swim in a river full of logs.

Once, when we were talking, Uncle Davy said that every rhododendron gives off a million seeds in dust. That there are places in Ireland where they war against the stuff—chainsaw the bush's flesh, then herbicide the things to death. You plant one rhododendron, Uncle Davy said, and you're in for an army of them. We'd been sitting in our schoolhouse chairs with our pots of tea. He was wearing his mustard-colored bow tie loose at his neck, had his lime-green apron on. He was polishing the acorns inside the turning of his hand. We were listening to old songs on the record player.

"The point of life, Lizzie," he said, "is to find the rare and to cherish it." These rhododendrons were multiples of multitudes. They were extreme biology.

They were a problem.

The clock was ticking. The Bondanzas were back at the snow-fort house, maybe waking up now, maybe calling for Matias, maybe forgetting, for one instant, that he was gone, maybe thinking that it was a nightmare they both had had, that Sergeant Williams wasn't asleep on the chaise lounge in the greenhouse court-yard, that my mother wasn't four hours away with her radioactivity and CNN on. That my uncle . . .

Well.

Every second counts.

I crouched. I unsheathed the machete. I walked into the rhododendrons, holding one hand out in front of my face and thwacking where I had to thwack, like Zorro might, like Tiburcio. My pack was getting slapped around by the thicket of limbs. I heard the pulse of my heart beneath the twisted *P* of my cap. I crept on, thwacking, heading up to higher ground, until I could feel the lean of the earth in my feet, and soon I didn't know how far I'd gone.

I kept trying to remember *Keppy. Don't panic. Mark your trail as you go. Keep your head upon your shoulders. Remember your purpose.*

The hill climbed. The earth went from dirty soft to rocky. When I forgot to breathe, I couldn't breathe. When I breathed, I swallowed bugs. Sometimes the bushes were so thick that it was easier to walk on top of them, like walking on a trampoline, springing from limb to limb, but that only worked for a little bit and then it was safer to hack back the thickest limbs or to crawl on the ground, where there was nothing but dirt and bare roots and sometimes a baby rabbit with its ears full of twitch, and the zing of a million bugs.

I couldn't hear a single thing but me in the rhodo-dendron grove. I couldn't imagine Matias out here, or Uncle Davy, or the Little Siberia men, but I'd smelled smoke, and it'd come from up high, and Matias had left me a sign.

MB.

60

I DON'T KNOW HOW LONG IT TOOK.

There are things I can't remember.

I was lost in rhododendrons, couldn't find the light through rhododendrons, thought maybe I'd die right there, inside the fist of rhododendrons, until all of a sudden they stopped. There weren't any more rhododendrons, and I fell. Straight into a pond. Water so blue.

Sudden sky and sudden pond.

It was like the rhododendrons had tossed me out, thrown me overboard into the muck and water. I took three steps forward and the water squished high, and I knew in that moment that there'd be no walking across this watered-up hole.

There'd be only going around.

61

I NEED TO TAKE A LITTLE BREAK, AND NO, I
don't want to see what's in your tote.

62

IT'S GOING TO RAIN.

Rain used to be peaceful.

63

I LIKED IT WHEN IT RAINED AT UNCLE DAVY'S house, especially at night, the summer before this. In the loft, Uncle Davy would hear the rain, sit up, and whisper through the dark: "Betty Boop?"

He'd tiptoe down the loft steps with his monster-size flashlight, throwing a cone of yellow across the room.

"I could use some company," he'd say. One pillow at my back, one pillow fluffed for his, we'd sit side by side, calling out the seconds between thunder rolls and lightning strikes, watching the crescent moons cry their sorrows out. The worst storms canceled the cicada songs. The squirrels stayed in their nests. The start of the fruits and vegetables knocked the back of the house.

Storms were the best. If they lasted all night, we'd stay awake the whole time, like it was a movie we were watching. Uncle Davy would start telling the stories of the cinema's greatest M-B-As as the storm simmered and raged. The tempestuous (that was his word, those were his people) Tallulah Bankhead and Joan Crawford and Greta Garbo and Mitzi Gaynor, Ginger Rogers floating out on top of a dance, Ethel Merman like a lotus flower in a swimming pool—he knew them all, a first-name basis.

"Oh," he'd say, and when the lightning struck, I could see the way he must have looked at the theater on the beach street where he and my mother lived. The movie stars were goddesses, mermaids, femmes fatales, fringed lashes, trouble, and after the show he'd walk home, whistling the movie songs, and find my mother doing homework at the table. He'd take out his pen. He'd sit and write to the stars. Once Judy Garland wrote back:

"Find the courage to be yourself."

In the schoolhouse cabin, inside the storms, my uncle's memories of the old movies flickered off and on until the rain stopped. We'd open the door and listen. Sometimes to the frogs. Sometimes to the sound of those white-tailed deer, running.

In the morning, when my uncle was back upstairs sleeping the stories off, I'd go outside and call my mom.

She'd be awake even if it was dawn. She hardly slept after Dad was gone.

And that summer she was wearing her hair in braids, the bottom parts of each braid dipped in green. She'd gone from that orange to black and now to these tips of green, like she could work the revolution of her life through the strands of her hair. I'd picture her as I'd call. I'd see her walking around with a porcelain coffee cup, her nose dipped toward the steam. I'd see her sit down with the phone when she heard it ring. Leave the cup on a sill. Put her knees to her chin.

"Lizzie. How are things?"

I'd tell her about the storm. About how the rain had hammered and the frogs had sung, how Uncle Davy was in love with Judy Garland.

In the loft of the schoolhouse cabin Uncle Davy would sleep. On the phone, talking to Mom, I'd watch the clouds that seemed to tumble down—the white chasing the black, and the white followed by sky.

"Lizzie," she'd say. "I got another no."

I'd feel my heart drop. My eyes burn. "I'm sorry, Mom."

"I can't seem to fit. Anywhere."

"You fit with me and Uncle Davy, Mom."

"Honey. I need a job. A real one."

She'd had one, or halves of ones. She'd had, ever since Dad left, a part-time life. Baker's assistant. Restaurant hostess. Receptionist for a landscaper. Cashier at Good House. Scraps of jobs, she'd call them. Nowhere-to-go-but-out jobs. Seasonal fixes. Never enough. The leftover employment. Mom wanted a real, full job. She sent her letters, wore her suits, drove into town—searching, asking, making promises—but there was always a better someone. Mom had started to see herself as the world's unluckiest runner-up. I was twelve that year, and I couldn't help her see all I knew she was.

"I wish," I'd say, "I could hug you right now."

"Yeah."

That was the year before this. In the weeks before Uncle Davy and Mom had their fight. Before I knew the word "estrangement."

The rain has come in.

See how it falls.

64

BACK AT THE SNOW-WHITE HOUSE, SERGEANT
Williams was calling in three possible kidnaps, but I
didn't know that then. I knew the pond was too deep
to walk across and that there were the eskers to one
side and petrified logs to the right, and I had to choose
a path and I chose left. The water sloshing out of my
sneaks, the cold mountain water up through my bones,
my heart like a stampede.

A pinecone fell from the shelf of a tree.

A deer ran past.

I ran and I walked and I ran and the woods echoed
slosh. The paths were weaving in and out, sometimes
thin and sometimes fat, and I kept having to choose
with the sky growing dark.

65

I DON'T KNOW HOW FAR I'D WALKED WHEN I saw Matias's cap. Beneath the overhang of a hemlock. On the back side of a rock.

The genius of my best friend, and proof: Matias knew I'd come.

Matias!

Uncle Davy!

I nearly called.

But I'd ruin any chance we had if I yelled their names out loud.

I reached the rock. I studied the cap, the jab of its bill. Over the gravel and moss, with the thump of the pack on my back, I ran, the cap like a flag in my hand. The first of the rain had started pattering down. It hit the leaves of the trees high up, and then it struck. A drizzle down my back.

I smashed Matias's cap over the cap on my head. I notched the bark of a tree and kept running. I notched another. The ground cranked and popped, and I could not see that far ahead.

Adirondack bears are black as the bottom of a burned pan.

Into the blackness I ran.

Over the mossed logs and smashed twigs, into the shadows, with the rain falling down and the mountain rising, I ran. Toward bears and maybe wolves I ran.

CNN. *Daily News*. The *Times*. They can tell you. How far I'd gone, how the weather'd turned, how my shoes had left my footprints behind, saddest things you've ever seen, stuck down there, in the mud. They can tell you the mileage, the acreage, the forecast, the count of bears, the tilt of the earth, the whole thing.

But they don't know how it felt to be me. And neither do you, though I can see that you're trying.

66

AND THERE, RIGHT THERE, IS THE NIGHT'S FIRST firefly.

67

WAIT, I ALMOST CALL TO YOU. BECAUSE YOU'VE left your tote behind. Because it will stay here all night, in this room with me, and there is nothing I can do about it. Nowhere for me to go beneath this rectangle of sky.

Not like I can get up, out of this bed, walk across the room, bend down, and steal inside the tote you left.

Not like I'll be able to do anything like that for a long time.

68

NOW IN THE MORNING I HEAR YOU. THE CAR door slams. Your feet hit the walk. The men who drive you stay with the car, quietly talking to each other. You open the door to this house. You walk up these steps. You are outside my door, and now you stop. You drop something to the floor, and it rolls around, it clatters. You turn, leave, and go back down the steps, all the way to the front door, and back outside to the car.

Then you turn, come back down the walk, toward the house. You come up all these steps, and you drop something else, and then you go back down the stairs.

The third time you do this, I can hear how out of breath you are, but you're done. Whatever you have brought here has been brought here, and now I feel you standing just inside my door.

I turn.

Your cheeks are red. You're still breathing hard.

—We're running out of time. It's my turn to tell you something.

Those aren't the rules.

—It's important.

I don't have to listen. I tell you when you talk.

—If you don't listen to my story, then your story will never make sense to you.

What happened will never make sense, I say. It can't.

—You won't know until you listen.

69

—HERE.

You pull five long plastic tubes in from the hall and dump them on my bed. Then you bend down to pick up the yellow tote you left behind yesterday.

Out of each of the five tubes you pull a roll of canvas, then flatten it straight. You lay each one out on this bed, side by side, as if they are a quilt. You pull the sixth roll of canvas out of the yellow tote and press it flat too, and it's much smaller than the other ones, looks a little funny on my bed. You stand back. You cross your arms. I try to push myself up, but then I'm stopped by all the pain in my legs and head.

The paint on the canvas is thick as Spackle and cracked. Each painting, I start to see, is of a single room, and each room is painted as if the painter is standing just outside a door and staring in. You can see the toothpaste there, the coffee mug over there, the diamond-tiled floor, the game of checkers, the bathtub claws, the dog on the rug, the stripes of paper on the wall, the smoking cigarette. You can see most of the things in each room, but you can't see it all.

Green is the thickest color and the green through the windows is the thickest of all. Green trees, green air, the green of the mountains far off, the green turning to blue, wild blue. The paintings are not really about the rooms at all. They're about what is happening beyond the rooms, outside, in the land of the free.

If I touched all that crusty painted green, I'd bleed.

What is this? I say.

—This is the story. This is him.

This is just a bunch of paintings, I say.

—Not just a bunch of paintings. They are paintings painted by him.

70

I STARE AT YOU, CONFUSED.

—Keep talking. You'll see.

Keep talking?

—Go back to where you were. Take me back. To your story.

71

I WAS CLIMBING THAT HILL THROUGH A STORM, that's where I was. The trees were growing thin. It was like the trees had decided to stop clinging to the dirt, so they quit and then all there was up there on the hill was stone. Big backs of gray rocks you would lie down on if it weren't raining. The rocks were like a game of dominoes somebody lost and tossed—everything fallen down and cracked.

The storm had slicked the stones. My sneaks had no more grip. The weight of my pack kept hauling me back, and even with the machete in its sleeve and Matias's cap over my cap, and even walking the way Keppy says a walker should walk—glide, Keppy says, and keep your knees springy soft—I couldn't get forward. The rain and the tilt of the rocks were bigger than any strength I had. My ankles cranked and popped.

When you can't scale the rocks, you walk around. I

walked the thin edge between the end of the trees and the start of the rocks, where the trail was green from so much moss, but also dark with mud.

A nest had fallen, and it sat like a lost hat on the path. I almost bent to pick it up and then I thought I heard a song—somebody singing far away in the rain—and I stopped. It was hard to see in the white rain by the rocks, hard to find the source of the song. *Nobody who is kidnapped sings in the rain*, that's what I thought, and what kind of kidnapper would sing—in any weather? I stopped and stood and listened. I was desperate for more signs.

Come on, Matias.

I'm coming, Matias.

Show me where to go.

But there was nothing out there, nothing but the rain and rocks, and I thought about maybe going back—down the hill, through the woods, down the slope, to the pond, into the mesh of the rhododendron jungle, past the rock, over the stream, toward the white house and the Bondanzas and Sergeant Williams and the news, maybe there was news.

But hours had gone past, and maybe there was no

news, and if there wasn't, what good would it all have been for if I turned around, gave up? The rain was really coming now—hard white slashes of it straight through my shirt, my skin. It felt like it was raining inside me— nails of the stuff through the ivy rash and the bruises and the scratches I already had. The earth was loose. The rain was falling down and bouncing back up, slapping me in the knees, and up ahead the path was splitting. There were three ways that I could go, and I'd have to choose. I didn't know what to choose, so I just kept walking.

I was practically right up to it before I saw it. Right there, on the ground, like a twig or a tiny tree root, but it wasn't that: It was a brush. One of Matias's watercolor brushes, laid down, arrow fashion, its brush part pointing to the rightmost path, and despite everything then I started running. I called his name, but the rain kept swallowing the sound. I ran until there was nowhere else to run. Until I found where Matias must have been going to.

The biggest cave I'd ever seen.

It was like someone had built a room out of the rocks and then the earth beneath the rocks had sunk down. Try to imagine a bear in the middle of a yawn. The mouth of the cave looked just like that. It was where Matias had gone, it had to be, and it was shelter besides that.

The air of a true cave is purer and more invigo-rating than any to be breathed on earth.

says Keppy.

The air of a true cave is not white slash. I walked as fast as I could into its mouth.

"Matias," I whispered now, because inside the cave my footsteps echoed. "I'm coming. Wait for me. Hold on."

72

I SMELLED WOODSMOKE AND BAT CRAP. I HEARD the hollow sound of cave drip and my sneaks talking to themselves every time I moved, every time I walked, and the farther I got, the darker it was.

Stay calm.

Don't panic.

I was wet to the bone in a damp place and when I turned to look behind me, toward the mouth of the cave, I could see that the rain outside was falling harder than before. Out in the acres my footsteps were being swallowed up. There'd be no trace of me except for the notches in the trees. And were those enough? Would they save me?

I had come this far.

Maybe that cave goes on for miles. Maybe it's a tunnel all the way to Canada and after that to the Arctic Circle. I didn't know and I couldn't tell and I couldn't keep walking deeper in. I felt the pounding of my heart. The sudden total tiredness of every muscle. I dropped my pack to my feet and slid to the ground. I pushed back against the cool damp of the cave rock and I tried, I really tried, not to cry.

It's just a cave, I told myself.

It's just a cave.

But a cave is a cave. A cave is spooky, creepy, bumps and slime, and I didn't know what would happen if I walked deeper in. I'd left my phone in Sergeant Williams's hands, just in case the kidnappers dialed in. I'd told no one where I was going. I was in a cave, a poison-ivy itch crawling up my arm, and an infection starting in beneath one of the Band-Aids the sergeant had put on, and what was going to happen? To me? Thirteen years isn't a long time to live, but it was starting to look like thirteen years was all I had. Because I couldn't go back and I couldn't go on, and the more I thought about it, the more the fat tears came. I was all there was, and all I had, and I didn't have a plan.

I thought about the cops out there in the rain.

I thought about Mr. Genzler and our butterfly boards and how much they would miss me.

I thought about Mom, needing me, and Matias,

stolen from a rock, and my uncle in his slippery shoes, and his rotten, no-good knee.

I thought about Dad never finding out how brave I had become.

Brave.

Get yourself together, Lizzie, I thought.

Be who you actually are.

I closed my eyes. I took deep breaths. I wiped away the tears. I thought of Keppy. "Listen to this," my uncle Davy had read just a few days before, when none of what was happening had ever been dreamed up.

"Listen," he'd said, and I remembered:

Instantly the unfortunate man is overwhelmed by a sense of utter isolation, as though leagues and leagues of savage forest surrounded him on all sides, through which he must wander aimlessly, hopelessly, until he drops from exhaustion and starvation. Nervously he consults his compass, only to realize that it is of no more service to him now than a brass button. He starts to retrace his steps, but no sign of footprint can he detect. He is seized with a panic of fear, as irrational but quite as urgent as that which swoops upon a belated urchin when he is passing a country graveyard at night. It will take a mighty effort of will to rein himself in and check a headlong stampede.

A mighty effort of will.

I inhaled and I exhaled, slow. I counted up to fifty. I reached into my pack and took the photos out—my mother and my uncle, Matias at the farm—and stared at them in the dull light near the mouth of the cave until I could remember being safe and strong.

Here's what my father taught me about courage: It has everything to do with who you decide you are. You may have your dad's last name, your father's nose, your father's ears, but you're not him. You may have 50 percent of his blood, but you can be 100 percent you. You may be told that you don't matter, but you can choose to matter.

And you may think that you're alone, but if you have courage, you have yourself to lean on.

73

—MY FATHER TAUGHT ME TOO. MY FATHER HAD talent.

Your father? Really?

—My father painted every painting you see here. Look at them. See? There's total talent. Beauty.

You think *that's* beauty?

—I did. At the time, I mean. Back at the beginning.

Even if they were beautiful, though they're not beautiful, so what? What does that matter? How does that explain things? How does that explain what you did?

—I thought someone who could make something so beautiful could be something so beautiful. That's what I thought.

You thought these paintings made your father *good*?

—I wanted to think it.

That's—

—I'm trying to tell you what I thought. I'm trying

to explain why I did what I did. You've been telling your story. Didn't you say I could tell mine? At some point? At some time?

I said I would decide.

—I'm asking you for time.

Time?

Well. Okay. You say he painted these rooms, all of these rooms here. Right?

—Yes. He did.

And you said he sent them to you? Or maybe you didn't say that. Maybe the news did. CNN.

—He got the paintings smuggled out.

And you thought—

—I thought he must have been thinking about me. That he was remembering us when I was little, when he lived with us in the house of six rooms. I thought it meant he missed me.

Missing you still wouldn't have made him good.

—People can change, you know. I thought he'd changed. I *wanted* him to have changed.

But look at these paintings. Look at each one. If your father loved you so much, if he painted them because he missed you, if he was thinking about you like fathers are supposed to think about their kids, if he'd changed, why aren't you in any of the pictures?

Why?

Like this one. This is an orange room with a blue table. On the blue table there is a purple dish. In the purple dish there is one half of one cookie. In the window there is green, lots of green. Forests and trees. There are no people in this picture. There is no you. *Someone* must have eaten that cookie.

Right?

And here, in this picture, with the claw-footed bathtub and the floaty yellow duck and the tiny wet feet marks on the diamond-tiled floor and the big rectangle of lawn outside the window. Who is floating the duck? Who is walking that floor? Where are you?

Nowhere. Right?

And where are you in this big striped room with the polka-dotted rug and the game of Chutes and the blue-green sky beyond? You're out of the picture. You aren't here.

This is your excuse?

This is why you did what you did?

You want to know what I see when I look at these pictures? I see a man conning you. I see a man already gone.

Your dad.

Because murderers with hearts of gold are real and true; I know it for a fact. But murderers like your dad: They're different. He painted these paintings to persuade you. He painted them to *trick* you, and yes, I'm sure, because look at me. Look at this bed that I'm in. Look at this room. I have nothing to do here but to think all day, to try to make sense of it, to try to see it as it happened, to try for *answers*.

Every scientist worth her salt will look for answers.

I'm worth my salt.

Your father sat there, in his honor block, where he shouldn't have been, with the paints he shouldn't have had, with the charm that wasn't real, while his murderer friend sawed a hole through a wall, some holes through some pipes, some holes through the steam they finally turned off. He sat there painting rooms you'd both remember, or rooms he thought you would, rooms from when he was your dad, and he sent them to you through a prison friend after all those years of sending nothing at all, and not inviting you to visit. He sends you paintings, straight out of the blue, and you think he's suddenly worth listening to.

You thought that what he'd made was proof of

beauty. You thought that beauty was proof of good. You thought that good was love. But you aren't in these pictures.

I watched the news. Your lawyer talked to me, the judge, the people who told me this story, who told me your name, who explained the victim impact statement. They told me you didn't understand the man your father was. They said you believed him when he sent you the paintings and the notes inside the paintings. They said he told you he wanted to see you like a dad again, out in the world. He said he'd done his time on the honor block in Little Siberia and it was his turn to be free, to be your dad, to know you, to be there for you. True.

He asked you to help him with that: to arrange a few things, so he could see you.

"Please help me see you, Caroline," he said.

And you believed him. You believed *in* him. He sent you paintings with colors so thick that if I touched them right now, I would bleed, and you should have seen through that.

Put the paintings all together like this quilt across my bed and all you get is a house. Tables and chairs and floaty ducks and things and windows looking to the great beyond, but no people. Six rooms. Six doors. Twelve windows. Your father put most of his paint into those windows, like he could slip free through them, run to the trees on the other side of them, disappear into them, wild greens and wild blues.

You thought he could be trusted. You wanted to believe, and I believe you. But he was painting for himself, for what he wanted, for what he thought he could get from you, the daughter he had left. The daughter he would leave again.

Aid and abet.

Criminal facilitation.

I know something about that.

Because your father's not the world's first narcissist.

Because narcissists, according to the pamphlets Mom used to leave around the house, only love themselves.

I read that, Caroline, and I read this: Narcissists only give you two choices. Give them what they want, or learn the art of courage.

There were sixteen hundred law enforcers out there. Eleven kinds of uniforms. Twenty-five hundred false alarms. People locked into their houses. Hunting lodges with open doors and bottles of gin and peanut butter. There was an uncle and there was a best friend and there was a girl out there, there was a storm.

It all came down on us because of him and because you gave him hope. Because you told him you would help him.

You can't take it back, Caroline.

You can't.

74

I WAS WHERE I WAS. I WAS STILL WITHOUT A plan. Past the mouth of the cave, the rain was still pouring down in thick white sheets, and inside the cave everything was growing darker, like somebody was turning out the lights.

Bears like caves.

Bats like caves.

Snakes like caves.

I tried not to think what else liked caves, but unfortunately, I remembered *Keppy*:

Transparent fish, white crayfish, cave lizards, white mice and rats, cave crickets, and minor species—all blind, and some of them quite eyeless—besides the usual colonies of bats.

You get a bunch of crayfish and lizards and mice and crickets in your head, the fact that they're all blind in your head, and you start feeling even more itchy. You start thinking that they're crawling on you, and that if you sit right where you are, your back against a rock wall, your chin to your knees, your body soaked with storm, you'll be buried in just an hour or two by all the blind cave things that'll find you.

Out there the rain was washing my footsteps away, my proof of my existence. It was washing away Matias's MB and his flourish, flooding the pond, smashing down on the heads of the rhododendrons, extinguishing any trace of smoke. I thought of El Cipitío, one of Matias's legends, the son of a curse named La Siguanaba. According to the story Matias told, La Siguanaba had been beautiful once. She'd also angered her god husband and so he'd gone and ruined her looks, given her a case of supreme uglies. Her son got caught in the fury of it too. This kid named El Cipitío. He'd never grow up, he'd always be eleven, he'd wander the earth in perpetual motion, wearing a large straw hat and a blanket too short to cover his belly. He'd eat a load of bananas and the ashes out of kitchens. He'd come into your house and leave a mess. But the biggest thing about El Cipitío was that his feet had been turned backward. Anyone trying to follow his trail would end up following that trail in the wrong direction, would end up being lost.

Anyone out there looking for me would be as lost as I was, and there I was, sitting with the blind things, waiting for a bear to rise up from the shadows. Black as the burned bottom of a pan.

With claws.

With teeth.

I needed something to eat, or I'd pass out with imagining it all.

I unzipped the pack.

Granola.

The sound of me crunching echoed for miles.

Then I stood up and shook myself off. I beamed on the flashlight. I grabbed the pack. I walked deeper and deeper in, my heart up in my throat, my pulse up in my ears, my sneaks squishing with every step they took, and with every flicker of my light I saw something people aren't supposed to see, even if their second-most-important hobby is biology. I saw bugs that were big as bats. I saw rocks that were orange, slick, and pink. I saw things that looked like stone that started, suddenly, to slither. I turned around, and when I looked back, I couldn't see the mouth of the cave. I couldn't hear the rain falling either.

And all of a sudden I couldn't go on.

I sank to the ground.

I sat on my butt.

I pulled my knees up to my chin.

I kept my hand on Tiburcio's machete and waited for a bear, and I didn't turn out the light.

75

THE BRAIN PLAYS TRICKS.

It tries to save you.

It tries to teach you who you are when you're on the edge of forgetting.

The cave dripped and things slithered and the remembering was vivid.

I was back with Uncle Davy, in my mind. Back in the schoolhouse cabin. Uncle Davy was polishing the acorns with his fingers, and there was a bowl of Cream of Wheat between us, a rhubarb pie in the pot-bellied stove. It was a TV studio afternoon, and there was leftover TV powder on Uncle Davy's cheeks, and it was the summer before this one, the middle of August.

He'd untied his bow tie and left it on his collar. He had his tangerine-colored apron on. He kept rolling those acorns between the fingers of his hands, and I knew something was coming, because things, lately, had been different. Things with Mom.

She'd call during breaks at the Tin Bar, but she didn't sound like her. She was talking about men and slurring her words and laughing too hard, and Uncle Davy wasn't laughing. He'd sit on that stoop, pressing the phone to his ear, blocking the sound so that I couldn't hear, but I knew.

To me, he said, "Your mom and I aren't seeing eye to eye."

"It's about the Tin Bar, isn't it?" I said.

He nodded.

"About her friends? The men?"

He nodded again.

"I wonder what you'd think of staying on at the cabin, Lizzie. After summer ends?"

I looked at him. I looked around. At the trundle bed where I slept, at the TV where we watched our shows, at the M-B-As. "After summer ends," he'd said. When Matias would be back in New York City. When school would be . . . I didn't know what. When there'd be a winter's worth of Deviled Eggs Express and so much snow we'd live in lockdown.

You can love more than one person best.

And I belonged with Mom.

"Your mother and I disagree," he said.

He arranged the polished acorns in a row like a fence. Him on one side, me on the other, the gingham tablecloth like a nubby map.

"Does Mom know you were going to ask me that?" I asked.

"I told her I might," he said.

"Doesn't Mom want me back?" I asked.

"Oh, Lizzie," he said. "It's not like that."

"What's it like, then?" I asked.

"Like trying to know what is best."

And that is when I knew that even Uncle Davy didn't always know about best.

I could hear them fighting after that. On the phone, late at night, on the stoop. Him with that phone in his hand, his side of the conversation, his words: "No place for a child." "Get yourself together." "What would she think about that?" My mother had no excuses, my uncle said. My mother was acting out against the past, against the man she had married who had left—my dad the narcissist, who'd talked so loud and so long and so much about himself that this was the value Mom thought she had. "Incidents with men," my uncle said.

They talked late at night, on the phone. I'd hear him from my trundle bed, through the door. Sometimes a firefly that had floated in earlier in the day would lantern up the room, go on and off inside the fractions of the seconds that felt like they were days or months, and I would watch and I would listen—and it was only Uncle Davy's words that I heard.

Then one night I heard Mom fighting back. I heard, I mean, the silence of him listening. Two days before I was supposed to go back after my big summer adventure, I heard my uncle struggling to speak on the stoop, and then I heard him saying this:

"You know that isn't true. . . ."

"You have to stop. . . ."

"I do know what love is. I lived love. Remember?"

There was nothing after that.

I waited for him to come back inside. I fell asleep before he did. The next day, a day earlier than planned, Mom came to take me from the six million acres and the schoolhouse cabin and the uncle I loved best. My mother, with a strange lavender stripe in her hair, and her clothes too loose, and her body too thin.

That's how I learned the meaning of "estrange-ment."

Nobody knows the exact minute of the exact day when cancer creeps in, but I can tell you this: My mother started feeling sick shortly after that. The lavender stripe in her hair turned to gray. Her skin went white as a frog's belly. Her fingers became so sticky thin that her one blue ring fell off.

She quit the Tin Bar. She would not call the doctors. She would not tell the truth. Pride or hurt or shame. Don't know.

She wouldn't call her brother.

But I did.

I was the bridge between. I was the one on the phone, in secret.

I was it.

And all that autumn, winter, and spring, while I learned more and more words for butterflies, put them down in my book of words, Matias didn't forget me. He painted postcards. He marked them *MB*. He sent them through the mail to me. Paintings of our rock. Paintings of our stream. Paintings of the sunbeams that rushed in through the trees.

From New York City to me.

Matias.

The postcards had no words, just pictures.

Matias, with his pictures, saved me.

76

I DON'T KNOW HOW LONG I SAT INSIDE THAT cave. Minutes, maybe, that felt like hours, with all that moisture leaking down, falling down—drips through both the caps I wore on my head, through my hair, down my neck, into the trickle of my collarbone. I'd be a stalagmite soon.

"Shake it off," I told myself. "Pick yourself up. Keep going."

I ran my hands up and down the cardboard of my soaked-through jeans. I felt the swelling in my ankles, the burn behind my Band-Aids, the poison ivy puffing up with itch, my heart beating hard. I reached into the pack for a banana. I peeled it down, ate it fast, tried not to think about the rats and the mice that would smell the sweet yellow smell, crawl up out of their holes, climb down from the tucks of close rock, scurry over the mineral veins, scurry over me, stand there wagging their spiny tails, waiting, and now, thinking about that, I couldn't move, and I reached into the pack for my bottle of water, and I drank half of it down, and I thought of how I'd been missing sunup to what was probably sundown and how Uncle Davy and Matias had been missing longer than that, and I was sorry, 100 percent, for the trouble I knew I'd caused, for the clues I'd missed, for the extra worry that would be rocking Sergeant Williams and the Bondanzas by now, for the call I knew Sergeant Williams would have to make to Mom, who was already sick enough, and this was all my fault. I shouldn't have had the hero's urge.

There are many kinds of courage, and some kinds are smarter than others.

I should never have hiked into the woods after that puff of smoke. I should never have sneaked off in the dawn. I should never have thought that I had any business out in the woods alone without a phone and without a plan, when Little Siberia had been breached by two desperate men on the desperate run, when all six million acres of the Adirondacks were on lockdown, other parts of the country too, maybe even Canada.

I was alone in a cave, and now there rose up the worst song I ever heard. A screech, a reach, a rush, a scream.

77

KEPPY SAYS, ABOUT THE CAVES, THAT NO ONE should try to explore one until she has learned how caves are formed. That to go ignorantly into such places is to court disaster.

Keppy, I wanted to say right then, *I could teach you a thing or two about disaster.*

But where in his book does it say what to do if you're me? If the night is coming on, if you've lost your way, if the mud has swallowed your own trail back to a rhododendron jungle you'd never actually survive again, if maybe the notches that you left in trees were not smart enough, not clear enough, not noticeable clues, and if someone, something, you can't see is screaming a terrible song.

Where, Keppy, does it say what to do?

I aimed my flashlight deep into the narrow passage, then tilted it toward the cave's rock sky, and that's when I saw them—the herd of little brown bats, their eyes like glass beads, their ears like triangles, their fuzzy bodies clinging to the leather of their wings, their wings folded up, their faces upside down. A thousand bats.

It was *their* song.

I stood up. I grabbed my pack. I felt dizzy, caught my balance. I lifted Tiburcio's machete and took a few swipes: *If you come even this close, I'll use this deathly tip, just a touch of the metal to the heart, don't try it.* Some of those bats flicked their noise at me and some of them tightened their wings and some of them showed me their ugly teeth, and I closed my eyes because I couldn't, right then, move, I couldn't do anything, and whatever was going to happen next would have to happen next. I could not choose. Then I remembered Matias and Tiburcio, how Tiburcio had been his protector, and so now I pretended that Tiburcio was right there with me, with his crushed hat on, and that he would get me through this.

I had come this far. I had no choice. I had to find Matias and my uncle. Both of them. At once. They had been here. And now they weren't. I opened my eyes and threw the cone of light in every possible direction and, deeper and deeper into the dark, I started walking, my machete raised.

78

SUDDENLY, FROM DEEP INSIDE THE CAVE, I heard a quick fluttering, then the sound of slosh, then the fluttering again. Over the hard beating of my heart, past the pulse in my ears, it was there.

Maybe someone running or maybe a bear, or a wolf, or maybe, just maybe, I thought, them. I beamed my light in the direction of the sound. I saw rocks toppled upon rocks, like shelves. Passages that got started and then stopped. Stone arches. The needles of stalactites. Guano. The farther in the cone of light reached, the narrower the cave became, but there it was again, a sound from the other side, and I was sure of it—somebody running.

The cave could have been a mansion of many rooms, and basements, and attics. It could have been shelves of stone where other campers had been, leaving things behind, little signs, a can of beer, peanut butter. In places it seemed like the cave itself was growing horns—hard nubs of mineral salts, not stalactites, precisely, more round, and every time I tilted up my cone of light, I saw the bats, their beady eyes, their leather wings getting ready to flap.

There were veins in the rocks, like Keppy had said. There was a small pile of bones, like pick-up sticks, and now I collected a handful of those hard white bones and began to put them down again, one by one, marking my path.

This way, the bones said.

Here.

Look for me.

Don't give up.

I stopped where the cave split into three low hallways of rock. I heard it again—the sound from far away. I stood there waiting, and now a huge white moth floated by, like two sails without a boat, a humongous creature, and I took it as a sign. I followed it into the cave's center hall. *Choose.* I did.

Narrowing myself through the narrowing stone, I felt the tug on my back of the pack and took it off, then I strapped it tight to my chest. I turned to fit my shoulders through the stone walk, and all this time I was praying out loud that I wouldn't get stuck, that the rocks wouldn't fall, that my light would not conk out.

The moth circled back. Changed its mind and its direction and floated just above my head, into the cone of yellow light, then circled again, back, as if to say, *This is the way.* I followed. The narrow passage in the cave turned and suddenly the underground world opened wide, took a breath, and right there, on the dark ground ahead, I saw two small silk trumpets—my uncle's spotty tie.

It was there on the ground, in a neat crisscross, like the trumpets were getting ready to be tied. Falling to my knees, I pushed the pack to one side, lifted those trumpets from the ground to my nose, and it was there—my uncle's smell—violets and M-B-As and brown sugar.

"Uncle Davy?" I said his name out loud.

"Matias?"

Their names doubling up on themselves and coming back to me in the echo chamber of that big room inside the cave, and now as I threw the light around in the dark, I saw the sticks of an unlit fire, two cans of beer, a jar of strawberry jam, and then: Matias's squirrel-hair brush, Matias's paints, proof that Matias was here.

My heart stopped right there.

Then it started again.

There was nothing else. No more evidence trapped inside that cone of light. My uncle and my best friend had left parts of them behind, on purpose, I was sure, for me. On purpose because they trusted me, because they knew that I would come, and maybe it really had been them, running. Maybe the escapees had forced them to run, but how could they run—my tall uncle with his slippery shoes and Matias with those hips?

"Matias!" I called.

"Uncle Davy!"

Their names came back to me in droves.

79

AND THEN THE BATS WENT WILD.

80

BATS, TRILLIONS OF THEM, GOING OFF LIKE A bomb, knocking their talk all around, squirming inside their brown fur and leather wings. The fur on the roof of the cave rippled like a rug being slowly shaken out. The sound was a crescendo that would not stop.

I went straight to my knees like the old-fashioned fire drills Uncle Davy told me about once, when he and my mom were kids in the Cape May school—*hands over head, this is a test.* I squeezed my eyes shut. Collapsed onto my pack. Crouched. Couldn't block the sound of it, couldn't stop that feeling of the air churning above, all those bats—one of me and trillions of them. I could have drowned inside the noise of it.

Will somebody please stop the bats?

Will somebody do something?

Please?

Courage.

My uncle and my best friend were together. Or they

had been and now they were gone, and I couldn't die there, on the floor of a cave, under the churning talk of the bats. I opened my eyes, and just as I did, I saw the bats leave their cave-roof roost and fly—out of the big room, toward the deeper dark. Flapping their leather wings and pointing their triangle ears toward where their dinner was, they flew and flew and flew and flew until I was alone and there again was that great white moth.

The back end of the cave, I realized. The bats had found their way out, and now I followed them, slipping the machete back inside its sleeve and putting the bow tie beside the watercolor brush inside the pack, then putting a white bone down upon the ground. I straightened the two caps on my head, so that both of the bills were pointing back.

This, at last, was my way out.

81

LIKE A LABYRINTH. FALSE ROOMS AND DEAD ends and passages too thin to fit through. So many going this way, going that way, getting stuck, until finally the dark inside the cave changed and the rocks eased up and I could see it: the dusk. I could hear the world again—the frogs and the bugs and the birds and, far away, the mosquito-snacking bats. I could see it and I could hear it and I was walking toward it, I was close.

The last of the day was out there, the actual sky, and I cried for the relief I felt. Put the pack back on my back. Walked forward, straight as I could, though the rocks were on an incline now, the floor of the cave rising up, making it all so hard, impossible, I thought, for my uncle and his knee, for Matias and his hips.

Where were they?

Closer. The frogs and the bugs and the birds and the bats, the sounds of dusk, were closer. I had to stomp through puddles and pools with swollen sneaks. My jeans were sandpaper; they itched. From out in the world now I heard a howling, like a wolf—*aw-wooooo, aw-wooooo*—then silence, then the wail again. *Aw-wooooo.* The voice was an echo of itself. The one *aw-woooo*, the next one, then silence, and I kept walking, maybe slightly slower now, up and almost out of the cave. I walked quiet as I could.

Aw-wooooo.

I knuckled my way into dusk.

I breathed.

The storm had blown off. There was a single fading thundercloud. The sky was an orange-and-purple drip of light.

The sky was.

82

AW-WOOOOO.

83

A WOLF, I THOUGHT, BUT IT WASN'T THAT. IT was the loon of the lake, my uncle's loon.

Where are you?

Where were they?

Where was I?

I didn't know. I couldn't tell. I still couldn't tell you now. The loons. The lake. The bats in the cave. And no sign of Matias or my uncle or the prison breakers on the pebbled beach or the driftwood seats, and maybe a wolf out there, and probably a bear, and all those bats with their beady eyes, and every sound I heard, every crack, every rustle, put my heart into a panic, my guts into a swirl.

A million ways that I could go, a million miles, and the dusk giving up and the darkness rushing in, and God Almighty, it was dark out there.

My last day on Earth, I thought. *My last dusk. My last moon, just rising.*

Aw-wooooo.

I had to think.

I sat on guard, with that machete.

I sat through the stars.

I sat through the break of the sun.

84

LOOK. LOOK AT THE SUN. LOOK AT THE SHADOWS.

There isn't much time for us now.

There's only the end, crashing down, coming soon, and I have to stop it. I have to tell you another story that's true. I have to tell you, again, who we were before this. The all of all of us.

Because it matters.

I was twelve. We were celebrating Matias, who was turning thirteen. We'd gone to Herbalish—my uncle, Matias, and I.

We'd had one cup each of cranberry tea. We'd finished off the bowl of salsa my uncle had brought—homegrown and homemade—and we were half into a slice of cake when Clarice, the former schoolteacher with a wobbly double chin who owned the place, came around with another pot of tea, pulled out a chair, and sat, smoothing the embroidery threads on the housedress she wore.

Matias was telling stories he'd already told my uncle and me, and he didn't stop; why should he stop? He had us laughing. About the candy shack his grandfather had built in the clearing at the coffee farm—the bright wrappers blinding everyone in the sun. About the sharks that swam right up to the piers where they sold the salted fish, and lounged. About La Siguanaba, the witch who teased the worst of men. About the antbirds and wagtails and nightjars and puffbirds that only Tiburcio and Matias ever saw; nobody else could see the best birds, he said. When he got around to the birds, Uncle Davy raised his hand, slid his sunglasses down his nose, and said, "Matias. That reminds me."

Uncle Davy dug into the pocket of his coat and felt around. "Ah," he said, "yes," pulling out what maybe you would have thought was trash—a wad of tissue paper, Day-Glo pink, so crinkled you could tell it had been scrunched up and flapped open a dozen times before.

"Happy birthday to the best nephew I have," Uncle Davy said, reaching across the table and putting the gift in the palm of Matias's hand.

Matias flipped his upturned hand around, like he'd been handed some sort of magic trick. He began to peel away the pink. Like an onion, Uncle Davy said, his hand already up to his mouth to cover the smile. Clarice had stopped fingering the threads on her dress, was rubbing at her second chin, was getting impatient for the big reveal and so was I, but when the tissue finally peeled away, she was the first to speak.

"Well, will you look at that," she said.

"A real M-B-A," Uncle Davy said.

"A painted bird?" Matias guessed.

"Nineteenth-century bird *whistle*," Uncle Davy said. "Moravian style." He pointed out the sgraffito, talked technique. He told the history of the earthenware, the Moravians of Bethlehem. The feathers of the bird gleamed dark black green. The belly was the color of cooked clay.

"You fill it with water," Uncle Davy said. "You blow right here." He pointed.

Matias nodded. Kept the bird balanced in the palm of his hand.

"Come on," Clarice said. "Let's see if it works."

She took the bird, stood up, went back around the counter where the cookies and the kinds of teas were kept. She turned on the sink tap and filled the clay bird with water, through the hole Uncle Davy had pointed out. She got a towel and dried the bird, then dried her hands, placed the bird back in Matias's hand.

"Do the honors," she said.

He found the blowing hole and blew. The bird sang. My uncle laughed.

"It's a real rare bird," my uncle said. "It's a real rare person who can get the bird to sing, first try like that."

I saw the color come up in Matias's cheeks. The skin around his eyes go brighter. His feet swing above the diamond-tiled floor.

"I have something too," I said. I dug down into my backpack. Found my gift in its newspaper wrap. The newspaper was thick and dense. It looked like a brick wrapped up like that, but when I handed the package to Matias, he laughed.

"Light as a feather," he said.

"Not a feather," I told him.

"What is it, then?"

"Guess."

He unwrapped some of the newsprint and guessed a spoon. Unwrapped more and guessed a ruler. Unwrapped again and guessed a vanilla bean. Unwrapped again and said, "It must be air. You've wrapped up air. A good-enough gift, I guess."

"It isn't that," I laughed.

Layer by layer, he unwrapped. Clarice had poured us more tea by then. She'd touched the bird whistle with a curious hand.

Finally Matias got to the newsprint's end. My gift rolled out. Clattered on the table. Somersaulted onto Matias's lap.

"Da Vinci Russian blue," I said.

"Serious?"

"Yeah."

He held the squirrel-hair paintbrush in his hand.

"It's kind of perfect" is what he said.

85

KIND OF PERFECT.

It was.

86

THE SHADOWS BETWEEN THE TREES BEYOND
the lake are not always bears or wolves or rats or
snakes.

The end of the world isn't always the end.

There is light before the dawn. The silver flash of
fish in the lake and the crackle in the woods and the
breeze blowing in, and when the fish jump, they are
the color of the moon.

It was morning, almost morning. After a night of
endless black. The clouds were pressing down on the
lake. The sun was leaking amber and pink, and now,
by the little light of the hardly-any sun, I saw footsteps
leading away from the lake, into the trees, into the
deeper woods.

Footsteps.

They'd been hidden by the dark.

I struggled to my feet. Cut across the pebbly beach.
Hurried toward the trees to pee, then followed the

footsteps up. Fast as I could, backpack on my back, chatter in my teeth.

Nothing, now, would stop me.

I was full of my whole self.

87

MY FATHER'S BLOOD IS IN MY BLOOD, AND YOUR father's blood is in your blood, and what you believed were the letters your father wrote you, the paintings he sent, the idea he had about you and him and Nova Scotia, being free.

What you believed is that he was not the man he was fourteen years ago, when you were four. Your father took a trooper down in total cold blood, no reason for it, just an afternoon of something to do. Your father swiped a girl on a bike with his getaway car and didn't stop. Your father had an idea about deleting your mother (that's what he said, "deleting," said the news on CNN), but she got wind of it, and who knows what he thought he'd do with you.

Your father was a bad man and he earned life, and he got lucky on the honor block, where they contrabanded him paints and a brush and some canvas. Your father painted his paintings and he got them out to you, first time you'd heard from him in practically forever, and suddenly he's there with his pretty pictures of those empty rooms and a bunch of stories about remembering you and he's asking you: "Come see me." He's in your life again, after so much time, and what you believed is that he could be someone else, that all he needed was a second chance, that if you loved him, he would love you.

That all he needed was you.

And a car.

He painted you paintings.

He was a stage 4 narcissist.

Don't think I don't understand, because I do.

But there are counts against you.

There is a sentence.

Nine months. Nine months of time you'll do. They gave you ten days between the judge and juvenile hall. You're spending those ten days here—restitution—and those days are slipping.

We're both the victims here, Caroline. We're two butterflies with our wings pinned to a board. I know this is true, I know he was bad, I know you regret, I know you are sad, but I don't know if I can ever forgive you.

Will forgive you.

88

YOUR FATHER'S FRIEND TOOK A HACKSAW TO the wall behind his prison bed and started to drill a little hole.

You could say that's when this whole mess started.

January, before my mother's cancer had been diagnosed, when she was just really tired, really crabby. When it was hard for her to clean the house, hard for her to talk to me, hard for her to go to work, hard for her to do most anything. Maybe cancer feels like being sad. Maybe it confused her. She'd quit the Tin Bar. She'd stopped bringing new friends home. She'd let her hair grow out to its natural dark and strands of white—the white she didn't expect, she said, but it was a good fit with her new job at the Sunset Retirement Village. She worked the early shift, receptionist, when she could get there. She spent more time on our couch. I learned to make casseroles, one for each day of the week, or tuna fish on English muffins, cheddar cheese with apples, or chocolate dipped into peanut butter, or lemonade from concentrate. On Saturday nights we'd drive to the Pancake House for our very big night out. And she'd look at me, with the gray beneath her eyes, and I'd look at her and think: *Sadness.*

By March, when I'd come home from school, I'd find her sitting in the TV chair without the TV on, her head thrown back, her eyes closed, her mouth open, the half of the house that had been furnished by my uncle's finds in a snowy drift of dust.

By April she hardly even heard me.

"Mom?" I'd say, and she'd open her eyes, blink, try to smile, run her fingers through the dark and white of her hair. She'd ask me about school and I'd tell her something about the names of archipelagoes or the state bird of Ohio or the art teacher who had been seen kissing the assistant principal or the butterfly I'd found, perfectly still, beneath a bush, and I wouldn't be halfway through most of it before she'd close her eyes again, put her head against the chair, pull her thin blanket to her chin.

"I'm listening," she'd say.

If there were pecan Sandies in the pantry, I'd get us some.

If there was milk, I'd pour us each a glass.

If there was something I could do, I tried to find a way to do it, but I was getting scared.

"Mail came," she'd murmur, when she really wanted to sleep. That was our cue. I'd stand up and go look for it, hoping for the best days, because the best days were the days I'd find Matias inside the coupons and the flyers. Those watercolor postcards he made himself—his paintings and his *MB* mark. Light on the rails of subway tunnels. Skyscrapers that climbed straight off the page. New York City at the hour of trash trucks. Yellow taxis in the snow. The library lions. People with long necks and window boxes with long flowers and the big BoltBuses that looked ten feet off the ground. And then, again, between all of that, the summer of our true adventure. The angle of every painting was tilted by the height Matias was. His paintings were his words. Every now and then, in the middle of winter, he'd send a painting of the coffee farm and the parakeets and the bougainvillea that was the roof of the house he'd left in Santa Tecla, El Salvador. He'd send El Salvador and then, a few days later, he'd send New York or the snow-white house in the six million acres, and I always knew what the story was.

I always wrote Matias back. Making pictures out of words.

After that, Mom still asleep, I'd climb the steps to the upstairs phone and call Uncle Davy. He'd do most of the talking, so my talk wouldn't wake my mom. He'd start in on the estate gossip, a Judy Garland memory. He'd talk about TV, columns, the snow that had fallen over the rhubarb beds and all those acres, and the white owl he'd seen, thought it was a snowbank falling.

When he asked me how I was, I whispered back. "I made the relay team." "I sewed you up another Day-Glo apron." "Matias went to Bryant Park for Christmas." "Maybe I will run for student council."

When he asked me about Mom, I'd tell the truth. "She's tired and she misses you. She doesn't like her job. She says it is depression, but I think—"

"Lizzie," he'd say. "How can I help?"

But we both knew he couldn't because Mom didn't want his help. She refused to answer his calls, she refused to open his letters, she refused it all; he wanted out of the estrangement. He had asked for me to stay on in the schoolhouse cabin for the year, and she heard the words like a betrayal. Like him saying she had failed as a mom, that she couldn't be trusted on account of all those friends, that I was better off without her. She couldn't forgive him for that. Wouldn't. Because I was what Mom had, I was who Mom loved, and maybe I was the bridge between Uncle Davy and Mom, but I was also the original reason for what had come up between them. I was the cause of it.

It wasn't until May that the diagnosis came. Not until then that Mom went to a doctor and got the news she hadn't seen coming. I came home from school and found the diagnosis there, hanging over Mom and the TV chair. Her eyes were glossy with all the crying she had done.

"Thyroid cancer," is what she finally said. Pills. The radioactive kind. The kind that make other people sick if they hang out too close, too long.

"I'll need the summer, Lizzie," she said. "I'll need a summer alone with the medicine. That is the best chance I have."

"Choose your summer adventure," is what she said. Tears in her eyes as she said it.

There was only one choice. We both knew that. She needed me to leave. I needed to believe leaving would help.

We both needed my uncle Davy.

I was the one who told him that.

I'm the one telling you.

Because yes, the people in our lives will ask us for things, and then we will have to choose. I chose to leave my mom so she could take the pills she needed to get better. You chose to help your dad carry out a crime that messed up the lives of innocent people.

Because, despite everything, we were. Innocent. We were, Caroline.

89

I WAS A DAY AND A NIGHT AND A DAWN AWAY from the snow-white house and Sergeant Williams and my phone, from the Bondanzas and their CNN, from my mom asking questions. I was miles I couldn't count, and could never track back, except for the bones I'd laid out like arrows. I was out of granola and out of water and out of fruit and my clothes were a crust and my teeth felt cracked from all the shiver in them.

By the lake of loons I sat. The sky was mostly blue, with clouds. The bugs were out—striders on the lake and dragonflies above it and mosquitoes I didn't care about anymore. I turned and looked behind me at the sweep of woods and the trail gone cold.

90

THEY'LL TAKE YOU AWAY, YOU'LL BE GONE.

You've shown me his paintings. You've told me what you've done. You say you had no choice, you want me to agree, you want me to say I understand and I forgive you, but the paintings don't help, Caroline. The paintings were how he fooled you, they say what I've said: Your father loved the green beyond the windows best, the blue breeze, the purple light he couldn't find in honor block, the wild blues. He stood at the door of your heart and knocked and you opened the door.

You chose your future.

You and a jury of your peers.

91

I'LL TELL YOU HOW IT ENDS.

92

THE SUN WAS CLIMBING. THE SLOPE BETWEEN the trees was steep. The rain of the previous day had left gullies, pools, little landslides, places where the moss had scrubbed off, mushrooms like chimneys fallen down. I looked for notched bark, boot prints, beer cans. I saw the sun between the leaves inside the shadows. A tiny bird with a broken wing.

The biting bugs hung low like clouds. I pulled the bills of my two caps around, tugged them down, forced the bugs off at an angle. I kept my distance from the darkest shadows. Sometimes the trees opened up onto paths of pine needles, and sometimes it was so tight between the limbs that I had to take the backpack off and hunch my way through, the low branches slapping me back.

So many crows and no bitterns and the earth kept rising, until finally I had to stop and look out and what I saw was like what your father painted through the windows of the rooms where I didn't find you. Green with blue and blue with pink and the kettles and the creeks and the till.

Somewhere out there was my uncle, who had traded an ocean for the mountains. Somewhere was Matias. And there was me, and ahead of me, the earth was rising still.

93

THAT'S WHEN I HEARD IT. LIKE A DREAM I'D had. Long. Low. Pushed out on two breaths.

One note. Two breaths.

Near or far, I couldn't tell. Behind? Ahead? Impossible. I dropped the pack, knocked off my caps, pulled the hair away from my ears. When the note played again, I was sure of what it was: the Moravian bird.

Fill it with water and it sings.

You have the knack for that.

One note. Two breaths. The song was out in the woods, rattling around off the kettles and the tree stumps, the snake nests and the shadows.

Fill it with water and it sings.

Like that.

If it was Matias whistling the bird, he was alive. If he was alive, I would find him. If my uncle was alive with him, we'd muck, trek, crawl slosh back to the schoolhouse cabin and the old potbellied stove and we'd call Sergeant Williams and we'd call Mom and we'd call the Bondanzas, and we'd be safe again. If. I slipped Tiburcio's machete from its sleeve. I lifted it to the sun between the trees. A touch of the tip to the heart of whoever tried to stop me now.

Don't try to stop me now.

There are murderers with hearts of gold.

The note was a song and it played again—two breaths, silence, starting in the east, I thought. The pack was on my back, the caps were smashed back on my head, the machete was back in its sleeve, and I ran. Over the knobs of stones and the thatch of grass, another fallen nest, my sneaks so blown up by then that I couldn't feel my feet when they hit the ground.

Where are you?

I'm coming.

No turning back.

The path between the trees was crooked and leaking and thin. I long-jumped the creeks. I walked the wet stones. I slid across a natural bridge of stone, and then I was running again and I didn't stop until I reached a waterfall that was spilling gently down over what looked to be rock stairs. A dozen stones going up and white-blue water running down, and far away, near to the sky, I heard the song again.

Where are you?

I'm here.

There was only one way up that hill, and that was by taking the stairs—walking into the gentle tumble of white-blue gush. The water went up to my ankles. The stones were slippery with moss. There were branches and little rafts of bark to walk around or through, and it was cold as the hotel pool where I'd nearly drowned, but I hadn't, and now my strength was coming back.

The hope of everything.

A dozen steps and then they stopped. There was a wide basin of rock—a kettle overflowed with water that had begun from some ledge even higher above. It was a straight-down rumble of white, cold gush, and the only way up was the pile of rocks off to one side— big and slick and sliced into by water and weather and winter ice.

Maybe there's always another, better way in the woods, but I didn't have the time.

Because time was that bird. The song I couldn't hear over the commotion at the falls. I had to climb fast, not look back, which is what I did—squeezed myself between the boulder cracks and the skinny starter trees and the sudden purple flame of wildflowers. My knuckles. My knees. Whatever it took. My pack trying to throw me back, the machete knocking around on the rocks, the spray of the waterfall in my eyes, and it was a long way up, and I could tell you how it felt, but you don't have the time for that. It's noon. The Dixie daisies died days ago. The blue moon won't be back this way again. I've seen the paintings and I've heard what you said and I reached the top. It happened.

I counted ten more steps before I slipped up onto a mossy path where a snake had left its skin and a stone stood and stretched—a turtle, I realized. The machete in its sleeve was like a sash against my chest. The knees of my jeans were the color of rust. My knuckles were a hot scrape. I looked up into the hollow of a tree and saw the yellow eyes of a saw-whet owl—the famous secret saw-whet owl—right there, watching me. It blinked.

Hope is the thing, and the Moravian bird had started to sing.

It was possible.

They were this close.

I was on it.

94

WHEN I SLEEP, I DREAM, AND WHEN I DREAM, I see it all worse even than it was. I see red in the blink of the saw-whet. I see the turtle like a monster Galápagos. I see the on and on and on of the trees like the bars at Little Siberia. I see me on the moss floor of the six million acres and I hear the one note pushed out on two breaths and I can't move, I can't stand up, I stay where I am, and the world ends.

I open my eyes and I'm alone, and I thought that if I told you the whole thing, start to end, I would bend the truth, peel it away, make the truth something I could stand—that's what the doctor said. Tell your story until it is a story, until it feels like you watched it on TV, until you believe it wasn't you out there in the woods.

Tell your story until the story heals.

I can't get my story to feel like that.

It hurts so much more at the end.

95

LISTEN: CAROLINE. I'M SORRY FOR WHAT HAP-
pened. I'm sorry for how many times you have had
to tell your story—to the jury and the judge, to me,
to those men who drive you here each day, who wait
for you outside. You have told your story and report-
ers have told your story. Your story keeps getting told,
over and over again. Everywhere you go, there will be
a version of you according to CNN, and then according
to the people who watched CNN and tell your story
in their own way. Everyone who hears your story will
have to decide if you can be forgiven, if your paintings
are a defense, if you should have been fooled like you
were fooled by your dad.

If you had a choice.

We're going to Nova Scotia, he said.

You can help, he said.

We need a car, we need a girl who can get us
there.

I am your dad, he said.

You aided and abetted. You took that car to that place on the map he had drawn for you—pencil lines on the back of a painting I've never seen because it lives in a bag marked EVIDENCE. He drew the place and put an arrow to it.

Sweet Caroline, he said.

You bought a Honda Accord with six digits full of miles. You bought it with your camp counselor stash. Twelve hundred dollars. Cash. You were living with your aunt. You had nobody to ask. It was April when he asked you, May when you said yes, end of May when you bought the Honda with every nickel of your cash. Three summers as staff artist at Sky Hop bought you that. Everything you had you gave because you thought he'd redeemed himself.

Your mother had abandoned you because she'd loved him once—she had loved *that* man—and you were the proof, the evidence, half his blood. Your aunt was a drinker, caught her Saturday fish, stayed to herself, and in that small room in the cabin in the woods where you slept there was darkness all day, the room closed in by the trees, the bears out there in the trees, the dangerous owls. You had no future in that cabin and no way to escape the darkness it was, or the fact of your blood flowing with half of that man.

I'm your dad, he said.

End of May, coming closer to June, you filled the Honda with gas. You bought two secondhand shirts and two pairs of thrift-shop jeans at the sizes he wrote in beside the map. You bought two jars of peanut butter and peach jam, crackers in an economy-size box. You stashed it all inside the Honda, and then the day of reckoning showed up. The promise you'd made despite yourself.

Meet them in the early dawn. Meet the two men who had crawled through the holes in the honor block and slithered through the tunnels and popped the cover on the manhole and stood up—waved to a couple and their dog.

Top of the morning to you.

Top of the getaway.

You drove the car to the promised place. You hunched behind the wheel and watched as, through the mist, two men trampled up from Little Siberia. Two men. One father. Down along the abandoned railroad tracks they walked, nobody on the chase, not yet.

In the valley, below the ridge where the car was parked, they walked. Hands free. Heads high. The tall one laughing, the short one catching the start of the sun on the gleam of his bald head, and now, just beyond them, somewhere east, you saw that couple's puppy running for them, wagging its tail like it wanted some fun, going up on its hind legs like a circus dog, yapping. Just a puppy with a wagging tail and a joyful bark, out for some harmless toss and catch. A cat-size mutt, no harm in it, at least from what you saw.

The bald man stopped.

Leaned down.

Scraped up stones from between the tracks.

He had aim like you don't want to think about.

One stone. Another stone.

All those stones, Caroline, that he threw at the pup. That little, adorable, innocent pup—long ears on it, shaggy coat, a red spot broken on its yellow fur. You saw it. You testified. You said. Your father, the one you tried to save, was stoning a poor pup.

And then he laughed.

You have said that was it. You have said, in the court, according to my mom, who went and listened, that's how you knew, how the lightning struck. This man out there on the tracks, in the morning mist, this man that you might have once called Dad, was the very same man that he had been when you were young and he killed a trooper man who was doing nothing more than filling his Crown Victoria with gas. Your father had pulled into the station, seen something he didn't like, and that was it. Murder in cold blood. No gold. No reason he ever confessed to. Your dad was that man, and he had no redemption in him, nothing but hate for everyone but him, and now that man, your dad, the one that you had come to save, was walking through the valley mist toward the ridge with the first of the sun crashing against his head, and a pup was hurt, and he wasn't a man you wanted as Dad.

He wasn't the man you'd hoped for.

You left the car where it was. You left the key in the ignition. The escapees were closer now, on the abandoned railroad line, headed for the ridge. You slid across the seat to the passenger side. You found the knife you'd slid into the glove compartment, just in case, an alternate plan. You did what you did, you heard the air sizz, you hunched and ran up into the trees as the men started their climb. You hid behind the thickest one.

You were out of breath, you said.

You were wild with the fear of what would happen next.

You watched. You saw how it was, how they climbed up the ridge, hurried to the car, got in, never even looked for you, never waited, not one second for you, sweet Caroline.

How they drove.

How they laughed.

How they thought they were as good as gone, too much ugly in them, too much boast for them to realize, at least just then, that they were driving on two flats. That you had sliced those tires straight to sizz.

You let them believe in their new freedom.

You let them believe they had won.

You couldn't imagine what would happen after that. How six million acres of the world's prettiest earth would shut down. How a Salvadoran boy with two canes and bad hips would be swept into the chase. How my uncle with his limp would go out there in his TV shoes and his bow tie. How I would come to the top of a new mountain and hear the song of the Moravian bird and keep climbing.

You couldn't imagine.

And you had left your fingerprints.

96

ONE NOTE. TWO BREATHS. I HEARD IT AGAIN. The sun had fallen into stripes between the trees. The earth had risen at its angle. The saw-whet blinked. I hoisted the pack higher on my back.

I'm here.

Horace Kephart would set off into the woods with his tent, his poles, his pegs, his canvas bucket and his spirit stove, his waterproof matches and his knife, and gladly not look back. He would go up against bears and snakes and lonesomeness, poison ivy, white cave rats, rhododendron jungles, and stand there, on the elastic earth, alive. He would go so deep in, get so twirled up, grow so dark inside the dark, but he'd look ahead. Foot-loose and free, he said. Independent. The man alone in the woods was a privileged man, seeing country no one else ever had, capable of more. Keep going. Trust the woods. Give the woods your heart.

I was a girl, thirteen years old. I am that girl still. I

was strict out of provisions. My jeans were boards, the bugs were mean, I couldn't see light for all the darkness that there was, and the only privilege I could feel was imagining what would happen next. I would cut the escapees down. I would find Uncle Davy and Matias—alive and mine and unharmed. I would tell Sergeant Williams, then CNN, all that I'd done, and because of all I'd done, because I was born with my own blood, because I am 100 percent of the person I am, Mom would get well and the estrangement would end and Dad would know that I wasn't him and I would have fixed every problem we'd ever had. Anything was possible in how I imagined next.

Standing on the angle of the earth, I felt *Keppy* at my back, in the bottom of my pack. I felt the weight of Tiburcio's courage in my hand. I heard my own voice inside my head: *Don't stop.* I walked through the stripes of the sun under the lurch of the trees, and when the breeze blew, the leaves shook and it rained, but just for seconds, again. Sometimes the light shone through the wheels of spiderwebs and I'd go blind, and once, when I looked up, I saw the white head of a bald eagle slicing through the sky. I was hot and cold and out of breath and I climbed, and right there, you can believe it or not,

I saw that fox again, the same black-purple raven in its jaws.

I saw it, but then it was gone.

Finally, again, the song was sung. The Moravian bird was closer now—top of that mountain, around a bend, where the trees were coming to a stop and the sun was falling more completely in and the bugs looked like a tornado funnel, the way the light was hitting them.

I didn't see next until I looked up again.

97

ONCE DURING A RAINSTORM AT THE SCHOOL-
house cabin, my uncle told a story. This was a thousand years ago, when I was twelve, before I knew what
I know now about hearts and how they will beat even
after they have burst.

It had been storming, too much rain to leave the
cabin. We'd marathoned a game of Chinese checkers.
Polished the gears on a clock. Made our own breakfast
hash, with crispy bacon and tender ham. We sat at the
kitchen table eating, my uncle fingering the acorns and
telling me the latest news about the Cream of Wheat
advertisements, the old-fashioned ones, which was the
subject of his latest column. Afternoon got to be evening. Evening got to be dark enough that he could pup-
peteer his stories.

He climbed to the loft. I sat on the trundle, lay
back, pulled the blanket to my chin. He powered on
the flashlight and bobbed its yellow lamp above the

crescent moon. He froze the tumbling dust.

"Once," Uncle Davy began, "there was a rain-storm in the woods. Three days of rain that turned the creeks to streams, the pools to ponds, the lakes into the start of rivers. All roads were flooded. All birds were grounded. The bats were stir-crazy in their caves. The frogs were stuffed into the hollows of the logs."

Uncle Davy flickered his fingers into the spotlight.

"Rain like that," he said.

He was all alone, he said. The mountains were slid-ing, the mud was thick, the schoolhouse cabin was get-ting clobbered by wind, and it seemed to him that it'd be but a short couple of ticks before the earth would become one unending waterslide. He imagined the corn whipping away, the tomatoes rolling, the cabin breaking loose, all of everything floating back through time. He thought it was the end.

"Then."

(In the light on the wall the shadows of his fingers stopped raining and six knuckles rose, three from each of his hands.)

"I heard it roar. Loudest commotion you ever heard. Like an old man snoring through a megaphone that had been slapped against my ear. A sound like that.

"You know what it was, Lizzie?"

I shook my head. "An earthquake?"

"No."

"An avalanche?"

"No."

"A bear as black as the burned bottom of a pan?"

"Bigger than that," he said.

Only one thing bigger than a bear in the six million acres. I knew it, from biology.

"Yes," he said. "A big bull moose with a six-foot crown of antlers upon its head and a bellow like the earth itself was speaking."

Uncle Davy could see it staring in at him through the crescent moon, he said. Just one eye, turned to the side, a profile glance into the schoolhouse cabin of Victorian finds, into my uncle's heart. The rain was washing everything away, but the moose stood, it didn't budge. Its face in the window started to nod, up and down, so that my uncle, sitting at the kitchen table, by himself, could see the forty pounds of mega rack, the flop of muzzle, the ridiculous bell, the big dark-brown face nodding up and down.

"I could see the moose but only in fractions," Uncle Davy said. "The moose, with its one brown curious eye, could see all of me."

Outside the rain fell down. Out on the porch, by the crescent moon, the moose stood nodding. One small itch of irritation and the moose could crash on through, bull its way through the Victorian finds, take the schoolhouse as its hostage.

But that's not how my uncle's story ends.

My uncle's story ends like this: The moose didn't leave until the big storm stopped. My uncle had been saved.

98

THE MORAVIAN BIRD SANG—ONE NOTE, TWO breaths.

It was out there.

They were.

They had to be.

There were long lines on my skin where the thorns had dug in. There was that poison-ivy rash, a hot spot beneath the Band-Aids, big blooms of bruises on my knees, and I didn't stop. I pulled myself up by the arms of the trees. I caught myself on the pebbly path and on the skids of moss, and when the slippery stuff or the slope pushed me back, I slammed forward, up and up, until the trees began to thin to barely any trees and the slope went up at a harder angle and I had to stop to catch my breath and then I started again.

I was so close.

I was so sure.

I was coming.

All the way up the hill with its moss. All the way up, the mountain growing steeper. All the way up, and then the mountain stopped short and flattened out into wide, smooth rock, and then the rock broke and there was nothing but a trickle of a stream way, way, way below—nothing but rock, then air, then water. I slid straight to the edge of the rock. Caught myself in the nick of time. Saved myself from tumbling over the edge, into the plunge.

I tried to catch my breath.

I tried to calm my heart.

A bald eagle sliced the higher sky.

A crow flapped.

It was so far below and so far across to the gorge's other side. I tried not to look, not to think about how many feet down—twenty? Thirty?—it might be. I thought my heart might stop, just imagining this. Suddenly I was lost in a crowd of butterflies—light and dark, blue and white. Butterflies, all over. When I could see past them again, through them, I saw, like a miracle, a stone bridge, like a delicate arch, like something someone might have carved. A stone bridge across the gorge, across the stream below.

One note. Two breaths.

I heard the song and looked up, across. I saw what I hadn't seen yet—an Adirondack lean-to, a landmark hut, just three sides and a roof. Left out there with a fire ring and a water bucket and a toilet pit, a camper's place to stop. The song was coming from that place where people stopped.

The stony mountain had been split and there was bridge between the two rock ledges, and if I didn't move fast, I'd be out of time.

Choose.

You get to choose.

It was up to me.

Over that thin stone bridge and a stretch of rumpled gorge, where there were logs and twigs and leaves, a mess. Over a smattering of spruce and pine and moss, a narrow clearing where the bright stream ran, and I was thinking about what Keppy had said, about the boughs of a spruce being a perfect, gentle bed. *Just get us all home safe*, I thought. *To bed.*

99

ONCE, ON THE BIG WHALE OF THAT ROCK, IN
the earliness of day, Matias told a story. It was the last
day of my first summer with Matias, and the sky that
we could see was cloudless, and words I didn't know
included "estrangement" and "vanish."

"Close your eyes," he said.

I did.

"Okay," he said. "Now you're there."

"There" was El Salvador, the coffee farm, the
weighing plateau, the breeze blowing through because
it wasn't coffee-picking season. It was Tiburcio in one
hammock and Matias in another and a canopy of
mango trees above their heads, the orange-chinned
parakeets chattering in the glossy green above, and
the coffee trees on the slopes beyond blooming their
white flowers, like jasmine, Matias said. The crystal
pool where Matias sometimes swam was down one
way. The ocelets were higher on the jungle hill. There

were butterflies like birds, the scuttle of an armadillo, a toucan's call. In the beauty and in the danger, my best friend and his best friend lay, Tiburcio's machete in its sleeve slung loose across his chest.

They were shorter than no one, and defended.

The breeze was rocking the hammocks. Matias was half asleep as Tiburcio talked, telling the Pipil story of the great Quetzalcoatl, the god of civilization, the force of goodness, the source of light, the serpent wearing feathers. Tiburcio talked and Matias remembered and still my eyes were closed as I imagined Queztalcoatl, who went down to the land of the dead after the fourth world ended and fought his way back up against the dark and turned bones and blood into man and woman, boy and girl, who is the reason for the beginning of us.

That's how Tiburcio talked and Matias remembered, and I sat there on that whale of a rock in the six million acres believing in bones and blood, the feathers and the sizz of us, the same strange place where we all come from. Quetzalcoatl, who became, Matias said, the morning star after his work was done.

"Open your eyes," Matias said.

I did.

"That's him."

He pointed to a break between the trees above, where there was one lone star floating above.

"The great god rises," Matias said, and then I looked up, then I looked straight across at the light that was Matias's eyes, his soft black hair, his smile—nothing small about him, everything bright. I looked at him, and that's how I see him now.

Perfect as the morning star.

And rising.

100

SOON YOU'LL BE GONE. SOON YOU WILL STAND up and go down the stairs, but I can't do that. I have four bones smashed in nineteen ways, thanks to your mistake, which was finding beauty in the paintings your father sent, finding the future in the schemer he was, finding a father on visitation days when you waited in line and checked yourself in and sat where he sat and he said, "Sweet Caroline."

Your crime was the hope you gave: "The car will be there, Dad." Your salvation was the promise you broke: a knife into the tire flesh.

Criminal facilitation with regret. That's what you have: your regret.

I have everything I can remember, and now I'm remembering the sound of the motorized bird that was chopping in just then, low in the sky above the six million acres. All those troopers and the National Guard and the helicopters swooping, and it had taken a day and a night and a half and hundreds of eyewitness mistakes and there had been a storm in the way, and Sergeant Williams was out in front. She had promised my mom, promised the Bondanzas, promised every other trooper, promised herself.

Some promises count. The manhunt was looking like a fan from up above—the troopers and the Guard curving through the woods, over the moss, into the caves by the lakes of the loons and up the falling water and into the shadows black as the burned bottom of a pan and out again over the bumps and hills. Armed and dangerous. The hunters and the hunted. The clock ticking, and three missing, and I was one of them, and Sergeant Williams was out in front, in the cockpit of a bird that rumbled.

I was on the bridge. On the skinny beam of stone that catwalked out from one rock ledge across to the other rock ledge, where the song of the Moravian bird was dimming. Even as I walked—my arms out for balance, my pack with its *Keppy* on my back, those two caps on—the song was going softer, one note, soft breaths. If I looked down, I would die; if I for one second stopped, I'd tip and fall, caps over sneaks, to the little slice of stream below, the frogs and the turtles and the logs, the leaves, the mess, so I kept on ahead. One step. Another step. Half breaths. My sneaks cutting into every inch I went and full of the squeak of the water still in them.

We are who we become.

Inch by inch. Across one stone bridge. From one ledge to the other. Like walking a tightrope or a balance beam or the thin last lines of a dream, and right then it happened, right then the fox opened its mouth and the black-purple raven escaped—flapped its punctured wings and flew, not enough height in those wings, not enough power. I heard the wings beating away from the jaws of the fox and the edge of the woods. The wings coming at me.

Across the ledge.

Toward the gorge.

Over the bridge.

I turned.

I fell.

Six million acres of earth. In a terrible scream of a rush.

My pack like a pillow at my back, a clump of leaves, soft twigs.

The stream a thin, chill thing.

The last thing I heard was the sound of the machete.

A distant, far-off clink.

101

WHERE ARE YOU?

I'm here.

Where are you?

Here. Here.

I opened my eyes in the stream of down below. I opened my eyes, and all I saw at first was sky. The whole big dome of it, the rounding blue curves of it, the little pokes of trees rising from the shined rocks of the cliffs, a fox stopped in its tracks, the freed bird flying. The earth is small. The sky is big. The sky goes on forever. The sky so dizzy.

I opened my eyes and I saw sky. I tried to breathe and the air coming into my lungs through the pipe in my throat felt supercharged and heated. The sound of the copter was coming nearer. The stream was flowing through me, floating off with my caps, stretching the curls in my hair, getting salty with the tears I'd started crying. My heart felt flat and wide against my broken ribs. My legs were smashed in wrong directions. I couldn't move and I couldn't speak and I couldn't come to anybody's rescue.

I closed my eyes.

I opened them.

The sky bobbed like a big balloon, but I could see now, up there, through the rough blur, the three sides and the roof of the lean-to. I could see it, but it was like seeing through smoke, like the shelter was swaying, like it was shifting back and forth on a pair of feet. I closed my eyes, tried to breathe again, tried to get my brain, my eyes, back into some working order, to stop the dizziness, to get the rock ledge and the lean-to to stay put, in one place, so that I could see what was happening, because the copter was coming in closer now, closer, and everything was rumbling, and there were little ripples in the stream, in my hair, through my jeans, through the pack, through the pages of the *Keppy* that had saved me.

My eyes were closed, and then my eyes were open, and despite the rumbling approach of the coming-closer copter, I fixed my eyes again on the lean-to, on the parts of it that were moving, and it wasn't the lean-to that had gotten to its feet, it was Matias. His eyes on me. His two arms waving, that Moravian bird in one hand.

Nothing small about him.

Everything bright.

Perfect as a morning star.

And rising.

102

THEY'D TAKEN MATIAS FIRST, A RANSOM PLAN. They'd hidden with him in the rhododendrons, waited to work out the rest of their scheme. No car now. Six million acres. The border to another country so many mountains, kettles, and valleys away, and they'd need money and they'd need a reason why no one would shoot if the law got in the way and they'd need a plan, so they took Matias, who had seen them anyway, who couldn't be trusted not to report back on the two convicts in the woods.

Me? I'd just missed them, my first morning out there looking. My uncle? He'd spotted them right away. Smelled the smoke and followed its trail. Found them long before they reached the caves. My uncle could have escaped in his slippery shoes and his spotted bow tie and his bad knee, but he would not. Wherever Matias was, Uncle Davy would be. That was my uncle's plan.

"You take the boy," he said, "then you take me."

"My nephew," he said. "My niece's best best friend."

Two were better than one. One was a celebrity. There were four now, out in the woods, and I was just behind them, and I was a full day late, but Uncle Davy and Matias—they knew I'd come for them.

They'd left those marks for me.

Through the rhododendrons. To the edge of the pond. Through the underskirts of trees. A night in the cave, with the bats. Out to the shore of the lake and up and through, over the wild blues and the wild greens, toward the mountaintop, up the waterfalls, across the gorge, Matias and my uncle going ahead, my uncle's TV shoes long gone and his feet bloody, and his knee twisted, and his body bruised, and his heart starting to work all wrong in his chest, his heart giving up, but not his hope, not his plan: Matias and Uncle Davy, to the end.

Four men. Two tall, two short.

They reached the gorge. They found themselves there, where the earth breaks apart. They saw that landmark hut, that place to rest, that place to hide, if only for an instant, on their way to Nova Scotia. Uncle Davy raised his arms like a cross and walked the elevated distance to show Matias how it was done. Matias walked on after that, his arms out, his steps short—across the stone bridge, over the stream and the long way down. Matias walked on, to the other side, to my uncle's arms, and now, in my uncle's embrace, Matias could hear the heart of my uncle giving in, how it was beating too sloppy and fast inside my uncle's chest, how it would be up to Matias now to keep my uncle safe, to use his brightness like a shield.

Matias and Uncle Davy—they had made it there to the other side. They had crossed the bridge, but now my uncle was hurting and Matias was standing guard, and now your father and the other began their trek across the split-faced rocks. Hands out, feet straight on the bridge of stone. Slow by slow. They crossed the gorge, like two hippos on a balance beam, my uncle said, like it would all go wrong if they looked down.

And that was when, my uncle said, he told us later, from his hospital bed, the sky broke up with a starry blast, a shooting star, like no star he had ever seen, like nothing he would see again, like something arrowed into the atmosphere from another time, another place, like something plumed. There was a force to it, he said, a sound when the brilliant light burst. There was a force, and then it vanished.

Just an instant.

Right as myth.

And your father and the other one looked up.

And your father and the other one looked down.

And your father and the other one lost their balance.

And my uncle and Matias heard them fall.

103

"YOUR HEART IS HURT," MATIAS SAID.

Helped my uncle toward the lean-to on the rocky ledge.

Helped him there, and the clouds came in, the rain, the swelling of the stream that would float the bodies of the men down to a place I could not see, and Matias wouldn't leave, and he needed help, and he'd had the bird with him, all that time, in the pocket of his madras shorts.

One note. Two breaths.

The only thing my best best friend had.

One whole night like that, in the lean-to, my uncle's head on his lap, telling the stories that Tiburcio had told in the hammocks of his country, El Salvador.

104

THEN.

Morning.

Then.

The sun.

Then.

Matias heard the fox bark and the raven squawk and the stream spatter up with splash. He heard the silent spin-spin-spin of his own Day-Glo cap. He heard the copter coming in. He crawled out from the shelter and around to the ledge, and he stood as tall as he could and he looked down and it was me in the stream, my arms, mostly my legs, like snapped twigs, and the running water running red. My head pillowed up on the pack, and the *Keppy* inside. The photographs. The rarest of finds.

"Glad for you," he called out, it echoed.

"And for you," my dry lips said.

If you thought books by dead people were just

something to move with the furniture, to dust with a feather, to stack your plate of pie upon, to give to people you don't love, you didn't know my story yet.

You know my story now.

The big bird with the helicopter wings was near. It rumbled in and pirouetted overhead. Matias waved his arms, brought it close, directed the eyes of the bird to where I lay, to the Day-Glo cap, the pack—the stream rippling through, my pack anchoring me in, my hair rippling out, like the rays of the sun, and the cockpit calling it in, and Sergeant Williams calling the Bondanzas, and the Bondanzas calling my mom, who was already on her way.

Coming.

Coming.

"Ready?" she'd asked.

I was ready.

I would be rescued, saved. I would be lifted up into the sky and taken into trauma and put back together again. Three weeks, four weeks, in the hospital, then ambulance home and then two strong men, carrying me here, to the top room in this thin house, where my mother made me a bed and someone cut a hole into the ceiling so I could see fractions of sky.

So I could see the blue moon, the morning star.

I would be saved. My uncle would be saved. Two floors down in the hospital where they surgeried me, they surgeried him. His heart is beating just right now. There's a machine in him that does the ticking.

Look up.

The sky can save us.

For nine months now, it will save you.

105

MOM WEARS A HAT ON HER HEAD TO COVER
her hair, which has turned all white, from the radiation
maybe, or maybe from the rest of this. You've seen her
when you come. You've seen her in the room where
my uncle rests. Downstairs. For now. He sends me
notes and he will send me notes until the day that he
can climb these stairs himself.

The fireflies have started in on their rev. In five minutes those men will come for you. They will call for
you, and when you don't come, they will come and get
you. But there's one more thing I want to say today.

It's this:

There's beauty in our world. Beauty bigger than
biology.

There's Matias and Uncle Davy in the cave, and it's
dark. The convict friends are deep in a drunken snore.
The bats are back and the blind things sleep and my
uncle and Matias sit side to side, and they're the only

ones awake—this tallest one, this shortest one, Matias with his crooked hips and his perfect heart. The cave at their back drips and slides. The bats squeeze inside their leather. The final embers from the fire fade blue to red to black, and it's dark, and they tell each other stories. Cape May in the fall, my uncle says. Santa Tecla in December, Matias says. Bird talk. Coffee smells. A boy named Greg. Tiburcio. Their words as quiet as frost. Their stories like forever.

It might have been dawn, my uncle wrote in his notes to me, when the white moth fluttered in. Dawn when they saw it, the two of them, this white moth breaking that black night with two bright wings of light.

"I brought the whistle," Matias said. "With me. I have it right here." A whisper so soft it made no sound.

Uncle Davy covered his mouth when he laughed. He shook his head, he says. "Funny thing is," he told Matias, "that I have another one just like it at the cabin. A rare-bird matched set. An M-B-A for you, Matias. I was waiting for your birthday."

"Anything happens to me, you tell Lizzie that she's my best friend," Matias said right then, tears in his eyes, Uncle Davy says.

"You'll tell her yourself," my uncle said. "Nothing will happen."

"Tell Lizzie," Matias said again, and Uncle Davy put his arm across my best best friend's short shoulder.

There is beauty in God's earth. There is beauty in the morning star that shines beneath the sun, that lights the loons. There is beauty and also maybe this: When I can walk again, if I will walk again, I will come and visit you.

106

I HEAR THE SOUND OF DOORS.

I hear the sandpaper shoes.

They're coming, and you are so tall when you stand, and I am, I really am, sorry.

Wait.

Stop.

Take this with you.

Matias would want you to have it, Matias would say yes, Matias knows you're here, I have written to him and I have told him. "She has come," I said, "and I am telling her our story, I am telling her about the bestness of you, about the star that appeared and fell and plumed, about how tall you stood and how you saved everything that mattered. I am telling her about our rock, about your light, about your bestness, I miss your bestness, Matias. I am telling her," I wrote, in my postcard to him, which my mother mailed—the extra stamps, the extra distance.

He would want you to have it. He knows who you are. He knows that you are sorry; you were fooled. Take it. You'll need a bird whistle of your own. You'll need a way to call out, if you need us.

Acknowledgments

Over the course of more than a year, I helped my father clean out our family home. Among the many found objects were the books Daniel D'Imperio, my antiques-expert uncle, and Horace Kephart, my camp-craft great grandfather, had left behind. These two men, the writers in our family, could not have been more different. But they were where I'd come from. Both are in my blood.

Every day, after working with my dad, I'd come home to my husband, a Salvadoran artist whose stories about Tiburcio and coffee farms and gold-hearted murderers have, throughout our years together, become part of my own canvas. I've spent time in El Salvador, beside my husband, his friends, his family. I've picked coffee with Tiburcio, eaten *pupusas*, and walked the jungle hills with armed guards at my back. I was once told to swallow my ring, so as to keep that piece of family heirloom safe as we drove along a highway. I was once whisked away to safety during rumored rumbles of coming civil unrest. I once walked estuary roads alone, photographing children who had climbed into trees. I once counted bullet holes in a wall otherwise gorgeously alive with bougainvillea. I spent fifteen years writing a memoir, *Still Love in Strange Places*, about my odyssey to understand my husband's childhood home—and I'm still reading, still learning, still listening, still deeply saddened by all that threatens that tiny volcanic country and still in love with the beauty and magic and history it yet contains.

Wild Blues erupted from an idea I had—an instinct, more than anything, about putting my mother's brother, my father's grandfather, and my husband's childhood world all together in one story. At the same time, news of a prison break at the Clinton Correctional Facility in the Adirondacks was ripe that first summer of first-draft writing, and while some of the details in this story were influenced by the actual break, many details, including the character of Caroline and the victim impact statement, are pure fiction. I was thinking about love and loss as I wrote. I was thinking about narcissism and estrangements. I was wrestling with questions: Where are we safe? What will we do for those we choose as family? Who, really, is a hero? I was thinking about those inimitable words of that most sensational bride, Jessica Shoffel: *You should write a middle grade novel.*

I thought I had myself a story, after many months of writing and rewriting. But it wasn't until I received a most exquisite eight-page editorial note from my editor, Caitlyn Dlouhy, that I could see what had to be done to make a very rough draft something closer to a story. For Caitlyn's immediate interest, her poetic notes, her kind encouragements, and her suggestive green pen, I am so grateful.

I was standing in an independent bookstore when I first saw the jacket art. John Jay Cabuay, we have never spoken. We didn't need to. Your work is spectacular. I'm honored to take my story out into the world wrapped up in your vision. Thanks to Michael McCartney, for the jacket design; Vikki Sheatsley, for the gorgeous interior pages; Jeannie Ng and Erica Stahler, for the copyediting; Elizabeth Blake-Linn, for overseeing production; Alex Borbolla, for the quiet and so-competent care; and thanks to Audrey Gibbons, for helping to spread the word about this story.

I am grateful to Karen Grencik of Red Fox Literary, who stepped into my life at just the right time. Honest and thoughtful, present and caring, Karen read not just this story but so many of my stories with astonishing interest and insight. She said, "I'm here," and Karen's being here has meant so much to me. It is also through Karen that I have had the privilege of working with Harim Yim, Claudia Galluzzi, and Allison Hellegers of Rights People, who were so magnificently enthusiastic from the very start.

I am grateful to Mario Sulit, my brother-in-law, who read not just as a Salvadoran, but as the court translator who first began to speak to me about victim impact statements—and then checked my assumptions against his legal community friends. Thank you, Mario, for your love, your spirit, and your enduring care.

I am grateful to Patti Costa, executive director of the Human Growth Foundation (hgfound.org), a nonprofit organization dedicated to supporting those with disorders of growth and growth hormone. This foundation is doing so much to advance our understanding of growth, and I will always be indebted to Patti for her careful read of the character who is the hero of this story—and for further sharing my pages with Dr. Joel Steelman of Cook Children's Health Care System of Fort Worth, Texas, who took the time to weigh in as well.

I have friends without whom this writing life wouldn't be half the fun, or have half the meaning. Alyson Hagy, Debbie Levy, Ruta Sepetys, A. S. King, Karen Rile, Amy Rennert—you. I'm lucky, too, to know so many independent bookstore owners, teachers, and librarians, and to them (for being who they are and for all the books they point me to), I also say thank you. To my students, past and present, from the University of Pennsylvania and Juncture Workshops (and also, essentially, the wise and most remarkable Jacinda Barrett): I'd be a different writer (and person) if you hadn't pressed me with your questions. I love the questions, and I adore you.

My father, named for that Dean of American Campers, continues, to this day, to support me in ways tangible and otherwise. My son, Jeremy, is light; he is profound; he cares. My husband, Bill, is my partner in all things—a man who, years ago, before we were married, sent me watercolors instead of words and now, all these years later, painted the watercolors for this book. He just kissed me on the cheek as I was writing this. "You're done?" he said.

Almost.